More in the Ranger Ops Series

She's tougher than he thinks. She's also more vulnerable than she wants to admit...

When it comes to two things—his special ops team and women—Lennon is never in over his head. But after a hot chick invites him as her date to her ex's wedding, he's not sure what he got himself into. He wants to see more of her—okay, all of her. Trouble is, he has no idea how to lure this evasive beauty between his sheets.

From birth, Edie's always been the underdog. Even her father didn't claim her. All her life, she's fought to get people to take her seriously, and in the tough field of journalism, that isn't easy. Fighting for what she wants is the norm, but putting herself in that situation still requires guts she doesn't always believe she has.

When Lennon discovers the woman he desires has so many buried secrets it will take some hefty explosives to shake them loose, he feels a little betrayed, slightly pissed... and very protective. He's not about to let her face down danger alone, but Edie doesn't need some chiseled macho man trying to break through her carefully constructed web of lies... or her heart.

Range of Motion

by

Em Petrova

Chapter One

"Okay, Hallie. I got out of my comfort zone by petting a horse, but this?" The honkytonk music blaring through the tiny bar had Edie stopping in her tracks. She looked at her friend, who tugged on her arm.

"C'mon! You'll enjoy yourself." Hallie managed to pull Edie all the way through the door and into the space.

"If a fire marshal got a look at this place, they'd be shutting them down," she said loudly to her friend.

"Don't even think about writing an exposé on that." Hallie hauled her across the floor to the bar. Every single stool was occupied. So were the tables. It was standing room only.

As soon as Edie thought this, two cowboys hopped off their stools and waved for the girls to take them.

Hallie's eyes glittered as she shot Edie a look. "See? Told you cowboys are nicer than other guys."

"All right, I might have jumped to conclusions." Edie's gaze fixed onto one hot cowboy's backside as he sauntered off with beer in hand.

Hallie took one stool while she took the other, and they ordered drinks.

Edie was feeling out of her element, to say the least. She'd busted her butt to get into a prep school, had won awards for her writing all through college and landed that coveted spot at an insider's edition of a newspaper as an intern. Journalism was her life, and it was hard not to look around and see stories... well, everywhere.

Her visit in the Texas countryside with her old college roommate was proving a culture shock. So far, she'd helped feed critters and stepped in things she didn't want to think about. She'd stroked a horse's mane and watched her friend ride around the fenced area.

But here at Big Mike's bar, things were getting up to Edie's speed. She eyed a man in a hat and shirt sleeves rolled over thickened forearms swig his beer from a few feet away.

"Maybe we'll get you on that dance floor."

She groaned at Hallie's suggestion. One glance at the line dance forming on a miniscule dance floor had Edie sweating in parts she hadn't known she owned.

Shaking her head, she placed her lips around her straw. "I'm not doing that. I'm not even capable."

"We'll see." Hallie had always been a bad influence—or was it good?—on Edie by forcing her out of her comfort zone. If not for Hallie, she would have spent her college years behind closed doors studying and writing pieces about the wealthy emancipating their children so they would receive a free ride for schooling. It was a valid problem, and one the public and financial aid agencies—

There she went again.

This evening, she was going to drop her pen and enjoy herself, but it was damn hard when journalism ran in her blood. Growing up as the only child of a single mother who was always out in the field to get a story of her own, Edie had a difficult time seeing life and not the work needed to go into it.

She swept the room again, drinking in the smiling faces of Texas country people enjoying a night out. Lifting her straw to her lips, she sipped the fruity alcoholic blend. Next to her, Hallie shot her a smile.

"Never thought I'd see the day Edie Howard was sitting in a place like this."

Edie made a face. "What's that mean? I'm capable of enjoying myself."

"It's not that—it's the country. I'll make our city girl into a down-home girl if I have to tie you up to keep you here with me." Hallie grinned, but Edie knew she was only partly joking.

Hallie had attended Texas A&M with Edie, but as soon as she graduated, it was clear she was returning

3

to the back roads she preferred. She'd rented a nice place off the beaten path and, besides boarding her horse and a pair of feisty chickens, she was running a flagship e-magazine out of her home office. She'd also asked Edie twice already to come on board with her, get in on the ground floor and see what they could build together.

Edie's dreams took a different path, though, and Hallie wasn't offended when she turned down her offer. She just invited Edie to come stay a while and she'd show her around.

Which included a stop at Big Mike's honkytonk bar along a road called FTM34. The farm to market roads confused the hell out of Edie, who was used to the disaster zone of the crowded I-35.

Everything seemed to be along a dirt road out here, though. Edie couldn't even believe this was Texas—it wasn't any Texas she knew.

"Beer." The guy at her elbow leaned over the bar to order, brushing against her sleeve as he did.

She looked to him and found him looking back.

Good Lord, they even grew men different in these parts. Maybe she was a country girl, after all.

Or she could be for this man.

Over six feet tall with the broadest shoulders she'd seen in person, he was not only built but beautiful. His features chiseled, hardened like stone.

He gave her a nod and smile and then looked around her to Hallie seated on her left.

4

"Hallie. Good to see ya." His Texas drawl was all maple syrup and honey with a side of grits.

Edie pressed her thighs together just from the sound.

"Lennon. Meet my friend Edie. She's visiting for a while."

He gave Edie a nod and looked her in the eyes. "Edie."

"Hi."

So lame. Hi?

She could almost hear Hallie's inward groan.

Okay, maybe it'd been a while since she'd spoken to a guy, and never one this hot. Clearly, she was out of practice.

"Where you from, Edie?" he asked.

"Texas Hill Country."

A smile spread across his rugged features, and Edie shifted on her stool as awareness stole over her. She and Jake had broken up months ago, and she hadn't gotten onto the dating scene since. Maybe it was time. One night with a cowboy like this one would smooth over any bumps she still felt at being jilted by Jake.

"Nice up that way," Lennon said.

"Lennon's a country boy at heart, aren't ya?" Hallie peered around her to ask.

The bartender slid his beer across the counter to him. He lifted it in agreement with Hallie's words.

"No matter where the wind blows me, I always will be," he said.

Edie raised her own glass and clinked it against his draft. Looking into his eyes, she sipped.

Okay, flirting was like riding a bike—she remembered how, even if it'd been a while.

Lennon looked over their heads at someone and did that sexy jaw lift thing country boys did in greeting. "I see an old buddy of mine. I'll swing back around and talk to you ladies again."

"See you later, Lennon," Hallie said.

"Bye." Edie gave him a smile and watched him move off.

"I think your 'hi' really impressed him," Hallie said.

Edie moaned and took a sip of her drink. "You know I'm good for rallies, picketing parties and attending long, dull meetings between men in suits. It's been a while since I've flirted with anybody, let alone a guy as hot as that one."

Hallie smiled. "In high school, everybody wanted Lennon and his brother. He seemed to like you too."

Edie chuckled. "Thanks for trying to boost my ego, but you don't have to lie."

Hallie gaped at her. "Didn't you catch the way he looked at you?"

She straightened. "Was he?"

With an exaggerated nod, Hallie twisted on her stool. "Let's hit the dance floor."

She caught her friend's arm and stopped her from hopping down. "Ohhh no. I'm happy right here."

Hallie eyed her and finally gave a resigned sniff. "Next time I'm getting you on that dance floor."

"Sounds like a threat, and I won't be bullied, even by the editor-in-chief of a new up-and-coming political publication. How great is it that you followed your dream and are already running full force?" Edie was impressed with Hallie's success, while she was still battling to rise to the top of the interns at *Notable News*. Long ago she'd realized she had to do a hell of a lot more work to get what she wanted at that place, especially since there were two men hired before her and the only other girl was magna cum laude from a big school back East.

Edie was always on the bottom fighting her way up the rungs of the ladder.

Hallie beamed at her. "I'm getting new subscribers daily too. It helped that you wrote that piece on my e-zine for *Notable News*. Thank you again for that."

"Of course. I'm just glad they accepted the extra piece after the story I'd written about Senator Arthur."

Just saying that name had Edie's stomach knotting.

7

For years, she'd found herself obsessed with the man, and not because of his political stance on gun control, which he was known — and targeted — for.

At the age of sixteen Edie had finally caught her mother at a weak moment and learned who her father really was.

Ever since that day, she had thrown herself into learning everything she could about Senator Bradley Arthur. Born from an extramarital affair between Arthur and her mother, who'd been digging into a story about the senator's political rise, Edie had no fairytale dreams of her father.

He had a wife and two children, now grown, an impressive mansion twenty minutes from his main office and a second home in Colorado, where he and his family escaped to ski in the winters. In summers, they went horseback riding there.

Discovering the senator had secretly supported Edie's way through the prep school she'd finally gotten good enough grades to attend, bought her peanut butter and jelly sandwiches and paid for her college tuition had stunned her almost as much as her resemblance to the man.

Not only did she have his very pale blonde hair — white blonde as a child — but she boasted his blue eyes. She looked more like him than the children he claimed... and she had never even met the man.

The past year or so, the senator had been targeted by anti-gun groups, and one in particular had taken things to the extreme by setting fire to his home, kidnapping his daughter and taking his nephew hostage, sending the rest of the family into the care of bodyguards. She was proud of her father for standing for what he believed in, but her journalist side smelled a story from a mile away.

Radical groups didn't usually set fires or take hostages—their goal was media exposure. Edie was certain the senator had ticked off the wrong rebel group and they weren't going to let it slide.

"The piece about Arthur was brilliant, Edie. Truly."

She beamed, thinking of how she'd managed to deepen the senator's story from what was typically written about the man. "Thank you."

"You're not afraid to state the facts." Hallie raised her glass to her in tribute.

If only her friend knew how afraid she was of stating facts—at least about her own tie to the senator. Maybe it was time to confess to her friend.

But how did one state that she was the illegitimate and secret daughter of a powerful politician who was rocking the entire nation?

"I like the hair. Why did you cut it?" Hallie's switch in topic was welcome.

Edie brushed at the shorter strands that skimmed her collarbones. "Just felt like a change, I guess."

Edie's gaze shot to that sexy-as-hell cowboy again. Lennon. He sure beat out Jake on a huge level, at least in the looks department.

Too bad it had never been about looks for Edie. When it came to men, she needed good, stimulating conversation, and Jake had inspired her with his knowledge of current affairs and politics, which had become her passion since learning about her parentage.

She'd been with Jake two years, and then he'd gone to a political rally and come back with the charming and lovely Miss Deep South or whatever her title was. Edie thought it was more likely Miss Deep Throat.

After a few weeks without him, Edie had realized a lot of what enticed her about Jake was that he interned for Senator Arthur. It gave her a chance to pick his brain about the senator and get to know him in a more intimate way than digging around in archives.

"Lennon's hot enough to make a girl sweat all the way across the room. Why don't you go ask him to dance?" Hallie nudged her with her elbow and then froze.

Edie looked around.

Suddenly, Hallie grabbed her arm. "Let's go."

"Wait, what? We just got here." She set down her drink before it ended up all over her clothes as Hallie dragged her off the stool and to her feet. They made it two steps before Edie realized what had come over Hallie.

She dug in her heels and came to a halt.

Jake.

And at his side, the blonde he'd cheated on Edie with. What were the chances he was in this part of the country too, unless...?

"Dammit. I knew I'd seen her picture somewhere before, and now I remember—Jake's new woman is from these parts. She won a few pageants, and all of us girls made fun of those pageant types. Ugh." Hallie dragged her a few feet to the side to avoid the couple.

Edie ducked her head, but it was too late—Jake had spotted her.

Hallie's grip tightened on her arm as he walked over with his new girlfriend in tow.

"Wow, this is like a college reunion. Who knew I'd meet two of my old friends in a place like this?" Jake had this way of talking that had gotten Edie going, and not because of his sexy drawl like that other guy. It was because Jake was smart, and she loved his mind.

But in the end, he was only a man, thinking of what was between his legs.

She slanted a glance at the woman on his arm. She was blonde too, but being a natural blonde, Edie recognized a bleach bottle blonde when she saw one. This girl was Platinum Number 006, by her guess.

"Hello, Jake." Somehow, she'd found a voice and managed to use it. At least she hadn't done any of the other things running through her mind—like spitting in his face, slapping him or picking up a barstool and bashing him over the head.

"Ladies, this is Emma. My fiancée."

Hallie's fingers locked on Edie's arm even harder at the news, but she shook her off with a note of calm and the sweetest Southern smile she could slap on her face.

"Why, Jake, that's wonderful news. Congratulations to you both. A long engagement, I suppose, while you finish your grad degree?" Inside, Edie was seriously contemplating that barstool right about now.

"No, actually, the date's set for next month. You absolutely must come to the reception. Baby, do you have one of those invitations in your purse?" He turned to his woman, who nodded and dug around in her handbag, pink nails flashing.

She pulled out a white envelope, and Jake handed it to Edie. "I'd like my closest friend to be there," he said to her.

P...U...K...E.

Edie smiled and plucked the envelope from his fingers. "Thanks. I'm in the middle of a research project, so we'll see if I can get away."

He chuckled. "You always did tend to bury your nose in the research part of your field, Edie."

"Yes." She twitched her hands into fists to keep from going back for that barstool. Her imagination played out her swinging for all it was worth, of Jake

12

falling over and taking his fake-ass Barbie fiancée with him.

Edie smiled, genuinely this time. "Hope to see you both soon," she sang out and then pushed toward the door.

When she and Hallie burst out into the cooler night air, Edie tossed the envelope on the ground and stomped it with her high heel. "God, I hate that guy. What did I ever see in him? It sure as hell wasn't his personality."

Hallie bent to pick up the invitation and stuffed it into her own purse. "I'm sorry we ran into him. I never would have placed him here at Big Mike's."

Edie straightened her shoulders. "Well, I finally got over that first-time-coming-face-to-face-with-your-ex-thing everybody dreads."

"Yes, and you were very composed. I'm proud of you. I would have hit him over the head with a barstool."

Edie burst out laughing. Hallie followed, and they headed across the parking lot to the car.

Before seeing Jake, she had enjoyed her time at the honkytonk, which surprised her. But seeing him had dredged up a lot of things for Edie, and none of them were about their relationship.

There was still a lot more she wanted to learn about her biological father, stuff Jake would know since he still worked for him.

13

"You know, Hallie, I think the country's growing on me. I might not try line dancing anytime soon, but I'll be back next month."

Her friend arched a brow. "Oh?"

"Yep—hand me that invitation in your purse. I'll be attending my ex's wedding reception."

* * * * *

Lennon eyed the woman in the checkout line ahead of him. She piled items on the conveyor—a rotisserie chicken from the deli, some strawberries and two bottles of wine.

Her pale hair floated around her delicate jaw like a cloud, and this wasn't the first time he'd wanted to sink his hands into those strands—he'd watched her at Big Mike's.

Seen her a couple of times in his dreams too.

She paid for the items and was just turning away, when he called her name.

She swung back to look at him, those big blue eyes fixing him in place. He forgot about the few items in his hand that his momma had wanted him to pick up on his way home for a visit.

"Hi," she said to him and then flushed a deep shade of pink that had his chest tightening.

"Lennon," he supplied.

"Yes, I apologize. I'm actually good at remembering names, except it was loud in the bar

14

and I might have had too much to drink later on at Hallie's place." She glanced at the bag in her hand containing the two bottles of red. "I'm really not an alcoholic either. I'm just refilling her wine cupboard."

"I see." He chuckled, and she did too.

He took a moment to notice more about her — the way her lips bowed at the corners, giving her a softer look and some freckles across the bridge of her nose. Looking at her almost made him forget his real reason for returning to the country that had less to do about his momma and more to do about his own cowardice.

"Lennon, are you checking out tonight?" the clerk asked him.

He knew the clerk too — he knew everybody in these parts, or if he didn't, he was friends with someone who did.

"Sorry, Jamie." He set the items on the conveyor and moved closer to Edie. She didn't step away, which he liked. Sometimes his size intimidated women, but mostly they wanted him for that very reason. It was true the shoe size matched what was in his Wranglers.

"So you're visiting Hallie again?" he asked Edie.

"Yes. She's running an e-zine out of her home. I'm not sure if you know that."

"Heard somethin' like it," he answered.

Jamie gave him the total, and he pulled out some bills to pay her.

15

"I'm a journalist, and sometimes she wants my insights on what she's about to publish. A second pair of eyes and all that. I hadn't expected to be here for a couple more weeks, but she persuaded me." She lifted the bags she held. "Well, she's expecting me."

"Wait a second. I'll walk out with you." He accepted his change and stuffed it into his pocket before snagging his bag with two fingers.

When they got outside the country market, he reached for the bag of wine Edie carried. "Let me. It looks heavy."

"Oh. Thanks. You don't have to do that." She relinquished the shopping bag to him and led the way to her car.

"How long are you in town?" he asked.

"That depends on how fast Hallie and I get through the material. A day or two."

He was out as soon as he enjoyed a country fried steak, gave his momma a kiss and figured out how to say goodbye to an old friend.

Forever.

"I see you're set for dinner tonight, and my momma's expecting me. But maybe you'd like to join me for supper tomorrow? There's a little Italian joint up the road. It's not very good, but I can promise the company will be."

She blinked up at him, surprise crossing her beautiful features. "That's very nice of you. But... I don't think so. I'm not in the dating scene."

16

Damn.

"Boyfriend?"

Whew.

She shook her head. "I'm pretty married to my career right now. I don't have much free time, and I'm not from around here."

He didn't say he wasn't either, or at least hadn't lived here in the past ten years. "I'm not asking you to commit—just have a plate of spaghetti with me."

A smile spread over her face, and his heart gave that same hard kick it had back at the honkytonk. After she agreed to the spaghetti, he wasn't letting her go without her number. But that was for later negotiation.

"C'mon. Hallie can't refuse you getting out and having a good time after you've done all that work for her."

She tipped her head as if considering her options. By his way of thinking, she had only one—and that was to go out with him, because he didn't often see a woman who piqued his interest, and this one had from the first.

"I'll even buy ya a meatball," he threw in.

The winning moment arrived as his humor hit home. She threw her head back and laughed. "All right. I'll meet you there."

Too bad—he would have liked to talk to her during the drive. But he'd take what he could get.

"Seven."

"All right, I'll see you tomorrow at seven."

* * * * *

Lennon was right—the food was terrible in the Italian joint. The sauce sour and the pasta sticky. She had gotten the spaghetti, because he'd told her it was the best on the menu. If that was the case, she'd hate to try anything fancier.

She twirled the pasta on her plate and brought a bite to her mouth. She tried not to wrinkle her nose as she took a bite. At least the company was good.

Lennon had told her several stories of growing up in these parts, how he and his brother had run the hills and valleys unchecked like wild Indians. She'd also learned a secret about Hallie's past she would lord over her if the time was ever right.

But she didn't think she'd be seeing Lennon again. The man seated across from her was… well, out of her league. Not because she thought poorly of herself but because girls like Edie didn't win guys like Lennon for very long, if at all.

Men like him took interest and lost it all in the same night—once they realized she didn't put out to just anyone. Only Jake had stuck it out longer, and she always wondered if it might be because he was trying to learn something from her.

"Hallie told me you've won several awards for journalism." His statement shocked her.

She set down her fork. "You talked to Hallie about me?"

"Yeah, we ran into each other after I saw you two at Big Mike's. What did you write about to get the top scores?"

She smiled. "The first two times, it was with articles that went against the grain. While everybody else wrote about current affairs or the pros and cons of GMOs, I was digging into much darker stuff. Hallie always says I make myself the underdog whenever I get a chance, and maybe it's true on some level. But I chose to write about things I was more passionate about than whether or not wheat crops should be enhanced for higher yields."

Lennon was completely engaged in what she was saying, and for the first time she wondered if maybe they had more in common than she'd first thought.

"I'm not much of a writer, myself," he said. "I'm more of an action kind of guy."

Looking over his muscles, she could see that.

"I did well enough in school, but teachers had to fight to keep me engaged. I bet you were top of your class, right?" He offered her a crooked smile that threatened to melt what brain she had right out of her head.

"Actually, I had my struggles too. My mother's also a journalist, and I was a surprise baby she didn't know what to do with. So I was left with neighbors and sitters a lot. Then awkward youth struck. I was bad at sports and picked last for every team."

"Known a few like that. It's tough on a kid," he said.

She went on, though why she was spouting all this to a virtual stranger, she had no clue.

"My grades were good, but I wasn't a good tester and landed in classes below my academic ambitions. I had a bunch of tutors."

"It's admirable that you worked for it." He took a bite of spaghetti and set down his fork. It was obvious the dinner was just an excuse for him to see her—he'd known how terrible the food was. It was a little touching, if she was honest.

"I did work hard."

"Bet you were the editor of the school newspaper too."

She gave him a small smile and nodded.

He sat back to grin at her. "I knew it."

She mused over the story she'd begun, considering whether or not to tell him that after she discovered who her father was, her late-night research had her grades slipping once more.

She'd been put close to academic probation, her dreams on the line. And once again crawled back up until she was on the top, which had gotten her into Texas A&M for journalism.

She stared at her meatball, listening to Lennon talk about how competitive he and his brother were in school and even still were as adults.

Now there was a confident man. That alone was sexy, but he had all the rugged looks to go with it. Plus, he was about as far from Jake as she could possibly want.

"I'm talking too much," he said, sitting back to sip his beer.

She smiled. "Not at all. What do you do for fun?" He hadn't told her what he did for a living either, but that was okay. He would or wouldn't—she wasn't going to see him again anyhow.

"I bowl."

Bowling? That was a little on the dorky side, even for her level of nerdy friends.

He chuckled, a deep, low rumble that swamped her senses. "I know it sounds a little dull. I promise I'm not a total dweeb. But this group of buddies I hang with meets up at a local bowling alley, and we blow off steam."

"That actually sounds fun."

"It is. Maybe you'll go with me sometime."

She wasn't committing to that—or the meatball he'd promised. The greasy-looking meat sat in the center of her plate. "I think I'd better get back to Hallie's. I've had a nice time, Lennon."

He stared at her for a long moment and then made shooting sounds like a fighter jet plunging out of the sky. "Crash and burn," he said.

Edie sighed. "It's nothing personal, Lennon. I like you. I told you I'm not on the dating scene."

"Well, besides writing and not dating, what do you do?"

"I work toward my goals."

"Which are?" He looked genuinely interested in her. She was flattered but still had no idea how things could work out between them, and she wasn't interested in dating to fill her leisure time. She could do that with other things.

Best not to get involved.

Though, Lennon *was* more of a refreshing surprise than expected.

He watched her intently, waiting to hear what she had to say. Okay, that was sexy too.

"Currently, it's to beat out three other candidates for the full-time position at *Notable News*. And to not let Hallie force me into country line dancing at Big Mike's."

That broke the tension between them as both chuckled. The evening ended with Lennon paying for their awful meals, leaving the waitress, who he knew from school, a generous tip and then walking Edie to her car. There, he leaned in to give her a peck on the cheek.

The brush of his lips spread warmth through her, and he straightened away before she could respond.

"Be honest with me, Edie. What's my chance of getting your number?"

Chapter Two

"Lennon!"

Before sliding behind the wheel of his old Ford, he looked up to see his momma running across the yard to him, a foil package in hand.

"You forgot your cookies!"

He grinned and closed the door again, walking to meet her in the yard of the house he and his twin brother Linc had grown up in. "This is the third pack of cookies you've given me this month, Ma. Are you tryin' to make me fat?"

It was also his third visit in a month. He sure as hell never believed himself a coward, and today he was determined to end that streak.

His mother reached him in a huff and grabbed her side as though she had a stitch from just jogging a few dozen feet. "You couldn't get fat if you tried. Besides, if cookies mean you'll keep coming to visit me, then I'll go buy more ingredients right now. I've seen you three times this month, and I can't remember the last time that happened."

"Thanks, Momma." He took the foil-wrapped cookies from her and planted another kiss on her cheek. She hugged him around the waist, and he closed his arms around her, still feeling the aftereffects of the bruises and battering he'd taken from his last mission with the Ranger Ops special forces team.

In his line of work, he never knew when he'd see her again, and he and his brother Linc always tried to visit when they had a free day.

She pulled away with a teary sniff. "I miss my boys."

"You should move closer to the city, and then we can visit evenings and not just once in a while."

"I'm a country girl and always will be. I'd never leave all this." She flapped a hand at him, shooing off his words like they were a curse. Looking over her head at the countryside—rolling green fields, wildflowers and the neighbor's horses grazing nearby—he could see why.

"Thanks for the cookies."

"Text me when you get home safe."

"I will." He kissed her cheek again and got into his truck.

He drove on autopilot, his mind and his heart back at the house with his momma. He and Linc had both been out of the house for enough years for her to make a life for herself without them. Her church friends and job at the hospital kept her busy. It didn't stop Lennon from feeling the age-old guilt of driving away, though.

He turned at the intersection, headed to the old cemetery instead of hitting the highway home. He had a stop to make, one that he'd been putting off for a while now. For weeks now, he'd come to the country with intentions to visit the grave, but he'd made excuses.

He lost himself in thought and didn't realize he'd arrived until he reached the grassy knoll behind the weathered country church. He parked the truck and scrubbed a hand over his face.

As he got out, he grabbed an item off the passenger's seat. The police challenge coin was one he and his closest friend, a fellow Texas Ranger, exchanged almost weekly on their bets.

Bet you this guy tries to lie his way outta a ticket.

Bet you can't get that pretty girl's number.

Man, he missed the hell out of Adam.

On impulse, Lennon grabbed the packet of cookies and carried it with him, crossing in front of the older section of the cemetery to reach the newer graves. He'd missed Adam's funeral because he'd been away on a mission with Ranger Ops and had never had the guts to come here before now.

The minute he spotted the grave marker and the name on it, he slowed his pace, taking the last few steps with his head bowed.

For long moments he paid his respects while moments they'd saved each other's asses played through his mind. As Texas Rangers, they'd come up against a hell of a lot of challenges, and it had bonded them.

Then Adam had gone out on a call and taken a bullet. Lennon would always wonder if he could have saved him had he been his partner and not off with Ranger Ops.

But there was no sense in wondering what if.

He squatted before his friend's name chiseled into the granite stone and held out the coin on his palm. It glinted in the sunlight.

"You win, buddy," he said softly. Then he took out one of the cookies and ate it. When he polished off the last bite, he set one of the cookies against the headstone, gave a nod of farewell and walked back to his truck.

Driving back to the highway, he took a shorter route through the small town. He needed to fill up on gas and could use a drink too. If he had time, he'd swing by Big Mike's, but the only reason he'd go there was in hopes of running into Edie again.

Since she hadn't responded to any of his texts since their date, he was pretty sure the crappy spaghetti had scared her off.

He was just climbing out of his truck when he spotted a pretty little thing with a flirty red dress swirling around her tanned legs at the pump across from his.

Lennon's heart jerked hard against his ribs. He hadn't expected to see Edie again, let alone after his thoughts had just touched on her moments before.

So far, his advances hadn't gotten him anywhere. He wasn't one to fail in the dating department, and Edie confused him. Maybe he'd come on too strong. He had to take a different tack—she was different from the women he usually dated.

Play it cool.

"Hello, Edie. How's your day?" he asked her in his best Texas boy drawl.

Her smile widened. Jesus—she wasn't just pretty but stunning. That pale blonde hair and her bright blue eyes had him trying not to stare too long. Her curves went on for miles in that red party dress.

"Well, I could use some directions," she said.

"Where ya headed?" He abandoned his truck and stepped around the pumps to speak to her.

"I'm looking for a..." She pulled out her phone and checked the screen. "A place called the Trinity Center."

Lennon let his gaze fall over her, taking in the red dress that tied around her neck and cupped her breasts to perfection, down to her tiny waist and to the hem of her dress that showed off her toned thighs. Her shoes were definitely party shoes—sparkly and high enough to display a lean line of muscle in her calves.

When he lifted his gaze to her face once more, he caught the gleam in her eyes. "I know the place. Wedding reception?" he asked.

She nodded, biting into her lip.

He didn't want to look away from her plump lips now, but he pointed toward the crossroads. "Take that east about two miles. The Trinity Center's off the beaten path, but you'll see a white sign at the end of the road. Take that."

Her gas pump shut off, and she reached for it.

"Let me do it." He stepped up and drew the pump from her car. "Don't want you getting gasoline on your dress."

"I've never heard anybody drawl the word gasoline like that."

His crooked smile was back. Something about this woman made him want to smile a lot, and he could use that right now, with memories of Adam so close.

"All the roads around here look the same to me. It's easy to get lost."

"C'mon. A smart girl like you who navigates the I-35 up in Texas Hill Country? You can surely master a few back roads."

When she smiled, he zeroed in on the bow of her lips and the shine in her eyes. The connection on his end was unmistakable, but since she had ignored his texts, cut their dinner date short and told him flat out

29

she didn't want to date anyone, he was pretty sure it was one-sided.

"Listen, you..." She cut off her words and tipped her head, meeting his stare.

He cocked a brow. "Go on."

"I'm headed to my ex's wedding reception," she blurted out.

He straightened.

"And I'd love to show up with a date."

Lennon dipped his head, fixing his gaze on her dainty feet in those heels. He'd like to unbuckle the thin straps and kiss the skin underneath.

He looked up at her again. "I'll go."

Her mouth fell open. "Really? I'm so relieved—I didn't want to go alone. It's pretty awkward."

"Why go at all then?"

She nibbled her lip. "I'm hoping one of our mutual friends might be there. In return for coming as my plus-one, you get all the prime rib you can eat *and* an open bar."

"Hard to turn down good prime rib." He scuffed his knuckles over his jaw. At least he'd shaved before leaving his momma's house and could pass as presentable. His radar was going off too, though. Something about Edie's expression had him wondering if her reason for going to the reception wasn't deeper.

"Could you like... pretend..."

"You want a fake boyfriend, I'm your man."

She grinned, and he saw the dark cloud over her expression wash away in a ray of sunlight. The woman's delicate features were made even prettier when she smiled—and especially when she smiled at him.

He wasn't feeling the deep pain of visiting Adam's grave quite so much now, either.

"The reception starts in half an hour." She looked him over again.

"I was on my way home from a visit with my momma, and I've got a freshly washed and ironed shirt in my truck." He gestured to his old Ford.

Her grin spread. "Then it must be fate. I hope you're hungry."

He was—but for round hips and soft thighs to spread for a feast.

She climbed into her car, and he finished pumping his gas and then parked his truck around the side of the convenience store. He reached for his black dress shirt laid out on the passenger's seat and slipped it on over his T-shirt, topping it all with a western string tie from his duffel bag.

He'd managed to score a second date with Edie— even if it was as her pretend boyfriend. What more could he want? He was getting an afternoon with a pretty girl and some prime rib.

It'd be enough for him any other time.

31

He ducked to check his appearance in the side mirror. With his best jeans and boots, he was good to go.

She pulled around the side of the store and parked. When he walked up to her passenger's door, she hit the locks just as he reached for the handle.

He tossed his head back on a laugh. Now this was a side to her he hadn't seen before. Playful *and* beautiful—a deadly combination.

Plus I get the prime rib.

She unlocked the door, and he climbed in with a chuckle, putting the seat all the way back in her small car to make room for his legs.

She brushed her shoulder-length blonde waves off her face and put the car in gear. While she drove, he focused on her legs and the sexy-as-hell high heel depressing the gas pedal.

She slanted a look at him, totally aware that he was gawking at her legs. "You didn't tell me much about yourself now, only a few things about your past. You just said you were headed from your momma's house. Don't you live around here?"

"No, but I miss the peace and quiet."

"What do you do?" she asked.

Answering that question was pretty easy when most women asked it. He always told them he was in law enforcement, which wasn't altogether untrue. He and his twin had both gotten starts as state troopers, then Texas Rangers. For a while, he and Linc had

32

been at opposite sides of Texas, until that day a bunch of Texas Rangers had banded together, and the Ranger Ops team had been formed as a division of Homeland Security.

For some reason, he didn't want to give only partial truths to Edie. He wanted to be himself with her.

This sure as hell was unusual for him—he took women to bed and the only thing he ever dwelled on were her skills between the sheets. He felt something with her, though—something out of the ordinary. He'd stepped into foreign territory and wasn't even armed.

He shifted position to get more comfortable and told her to take a left at the sign.

"I work for a government agency." He didn't even like giving her the half-truth, but it was the closest he could come to the full story.

"Sounds interesting."

Before she could ask more, he changed the topic of conversation, steering it away from himself.

"What's our story?" he asked.

She glanced at him, those baby blues taking all his focus. "I hadn't thought up one. What do you think?"

"Met on the job. I was fixin' the office lights and you couldn't stop staring at me on the ladder near your desk."

She giggled. "Should I be worried at how quickly you came up with that? Are you a compulsive liar or something?"

"No. Just used to thinking on the fly."

"That's a relief. I was worried you've done this before."

"Well, I am in the business of rescuing damsels in distress."

She sent him a long look as they bumped down the gravel road leading to the country barn that served as a reception center. "I'm not a damsel. But I can't wait to see Jake's face when I walk in with you, cowboy."

* * * * *

She must be crazy. She'd only come to Jake's reception hoping that Senator Arthur was attending too. Surely, her ex would have invited him, and the way Jake talked, they were close friends.

Was she really ready to come face-to-face with her biological father? She'd given this some long, hard thought and still didn't know what she wanted to get out of meeting the senator.

Maybe it was some deep-rooted childhood daddy issues, always dreaming of her father seeing her and apologizing for not being there her entire life.

Of not claiming her.

She suddenly had the jitters. Maybe she was stupid for coming.

Sweeping her gaze around the room yet again, she lingered over all the blond men. Not one had the tall physique of Senator Arthur. He wasn't here yet.

The place was filling up fast, and the large barn was actually a charming venue. She was surprised Jake would allow himself to be countrified, but she could see him wanting to please his new Barbie doll pageant queen bride.

The barnwood floors and high beams were where the country aspect of the reception ended, though. Small tables were covered in white linen, china and glassware as delicate as soap bubbles. The centerpieces must have cost hundreds of dollars each. In the corner wasn't a country band with fiddle and banjo but a string quartet playing classical music at the moment.

The bride and groom had already made their entrance to much applause, and Edie clapped along with the rest of them, including Lennon. The man sat beside her, his pose relaxed. It was hot inside the building, and he had rolled his black dress shirt over his forearms, giving her an enticing view of tendons and veins snaking up under the cuffs.

Each time he brought his whiskey to his lips, she had to stifle a shiver of arousal.

Every other woman in the place was staring at Lennon too. She'd caught a few of the bolder ones giving him winks and smiles, but Lennon only returned their interest with a single nod of greeting.

He was definitely playing the devoted boyfriend, and Edie was grateful for it.

After a couple speeches from various wedding party members, dinner was announced. Everybody got up to head to the buffet, and Lennon seemed to be a pro at this part of the game, because he jumped up, grabbed Edie by the arm and steered her to the head of the line.

"How did you do that?" she whispered as he edged in front of a group of people.

"Easy. Give them the country smile." He delivered it now, and she had to admit, it dazzled her with white teeth and creases around his hazel eyes.

She nodded dumbly and accepted the plate he put into her hands for her to fill.

She continued looking all around, checking the entrance over and over again for a glimpse of the senator, but he still wasn't there when they took their seats at the table again to eat.

"I must say you delivered on the prime rib promise," he drawled, knife and fork in hand. Even the way he held his fork was sexy, with the tines down.

A waiter came around asking if anybody wanted another drink, and she ordered a rum and Coke, though she had to watch herself. More than two drinks would lower her inhibitions, and she was already in danger of stripping off all her clothes for her sexy date. Watching the man eat prime rib and shoot back whiskey was hot enough, but did he have to look at her that way too? Like he'd eat her up next?

Maybe she'd made a mistake in saying no dating and then asking him to accompany her.

Maybe it was the texts he'd sent that she never answered. All of it was wearing her down. Either that, or it was the combination of his muscles and the rum.

"What would you have done if the prime rib wasn't any good?" she asked.

He cocked a brow at her. "You'd have to pay me in dances. Actually, I think that's part of the act, don't you?"

"I don't dance," she said.

"We'll see." He grinned around another bite of meat.

After she'd picked at her meal, she realized she needed to soak up any alcohol in her stomach in case the senator did show up. After all, she couldn't start spouting drunken accusations at him for abandoning her. So she buttered her dinner roll and picked it apart in pieces, popping each into her mouth.

Lennon was watching her with interest, his gaze dropping to her lips and lingering there before moving back to her fingers.

Her stomach swirled with a little warmth from the alcohol and a hell of a lot of attraction.

"How is it you don't have a girlfriend?" she blurted out.

"Guess I haven't met anybody worth keepin' around." His stare fixed on hers for several long heartbeats.

The bridal dance was announced, and then the dance floor flooded with couples. The senator was not among them. It was clear he wasn't coming. And Edie didn't know whether to be relieved or disappointed.

She was just considering whether or not her blood alcohol level was too high to leave the reception, when Lennon stood and took her by the hand. "Let's dance."

A shiver ran through her at the rumble of his deep voice.

He led her onto the dance floor. The bride and groom stood not far off, dancing awkwardly like there was a wedge between them, but Lennon hooked her around the waist and yanked Edie flush against him.

When he started to bump and grind in time to the music, Edie's body caught on fire. The flames spreading through her groin must be from the rum and Cokes, right?

He shot a look over her head. "Your ex is lookin' this way." Without another word, Lennon kissed her.

And it was no soft brushing of lips. It was a claiming, all-consuming, openmouthed display that left her panting and she hoped her ex questioning his life right now.

He tore his lips away.

"That wasn't part of the deal," she said shakily.

His crooked grin cut a path up his cheek. "Did you mind it?"

She could only shake her head no, too turned on from the unplanned kiss. Actually, it had been the hottest kiss of her life.

She forgot about Jake or her father the senator who hadn't shown up. Right now, she was in the arms of a very hot, intriguing cowboy who had enough moves to render her stupid. Between his tight grip on her hips and the shake of his ass to the next fast country song, Edie sure was drooling.

Every other woman in the place was staring at Lennon too, and no wonder. Looking at him felt like sinning. Dressed in slick black, a worn hat and boots, with his muscles popping out whenever he so much as flicked a finger and a crooked smile that hit a female right in all the lady parts, he was one hell of a fine specimen of manhood.

Finding him at the gas pump was the best luck she'd had in... well, ages.

Lennon stared deep into her eyes.

Too deep.

She wasn't prepared for the odd mixture of feelings he stirred up inside her.

"What are you thinking?" His voice was gritty.

She didn't need any entanglements. "No strings," she told him.

She meant what she said—she wasn't in the market for a relationship right now. Focusing on her internship and making it into a full-time position with *Notable News* was more than enough.

But... it had been so long since she'd let a man touch her this way, and she was practically gagging for more of it from Lennon.

The song switched back to a slow number. Lennon swooped her up against him even tighter, so not even a breath of air could shimmy between their bodies.

He whirled her, and she giggled.

"Having a good time?" he asked, low.

She planted a hand on his shoulder. "Actually, yes."

"You sound surprised."

"Does anybody go to an ex's wedding and enjoy themselves?"

When he gave that crooked smile, she was sucked right in. Looking closer at his face, she saw his nose had been broken before and bore a bump on the bridge. He also had a scar through one brow and on a cheekbone. His little imperfections only lent to his rugged appearance, though.

"Would you go to an ex's wedding?" she asked.

"Never kept in touch with any to be invited." He whirled her, and all eyes were on them.

Lennon didn't seem to notice at all, though, attention only on her.

"I have a confession to make, Edie." His stare drilled into her, and she forgot she had feet, but he continued to move her around the dance floor between couples.

"What is it?" She sounded so breathless.

"I wasn't kissin' you for show." To prove his point, he moved in and captured her mouth again. She stopped moving and put her arms around his neck, and he planted a hand on her lower back.

Desire shot through her entire body, and the world flowed away. She tumbled into forbidden territory for a long minute before dragging her mouth from his.

She stared up at him, chest heaving for air.

"Let's go outside for a bit," he said.

Exactly what she'd been thinking.

Or was that the two drinks talking? Two wasn't a lot, and she felt as if she had all her faculties, though she definitely wouldn't drive quite yet.

Which meant she had some time before she could leave...

She nodded and slipped her hand into Lennon's. He crushed her fingers lightly in his rough grip as he wove his way off the dance floor, past the staring newlyweds and straight out the door.

The day was hot, but the country venue offered some shady spots, and Lennon headed for one.

Her heels threatened to twist out from under her, and she drew to a stop. He tossed a look back at her, and she saw determination and desire stamped all over his handsome face. Her stomach tingled.

"My heels," she said.

He bent and flicked the tiny buckle of one before sliding it off her foot. Then the other.

She could do nothing but stare at him, shocked he had managed the small buckles with such big hands.

Speaking of big hands... he had big feet too. Did that mean—?

"C'mon," he rasped out and took her by the hand again. They crossed the grounds where the chairs from the wedding ceremony she hadn't actually attended were being folded and loaded onto a truck to return to storage for the next nuptials. The land sloped downward, and she was grateful not to be wearing shoes right now, as she'd have a broken ankle. Lennon carried both her heels by the straps in his other hand, and it gave Edie a strange ripple in her stomach to know he cared enough to do it.

He let her go long enough to hold a branch for her, and she ducked beneath it. Her hair caught on a small bit of the branch, and he reached up to tug it free with the utmost tenderness. She gaped at him. Who was this man?

If he was pulling out a bag of tricks with seduction in mind, he had one hell of a stash and knew how to use it too.

He tossed a look at her. "All right?"

"Yes." Her answer came out whisper soft.

The corner of his lips quirked again before he faced forward and continued down a small slope. To her surprise, a creek flowed through the land, cutting a zigzag path.

"Did you know this was here?"

"Never been here before. But I heard the water."

"You heard the water. How the heck? Who are you?"

"I'm country," he said, though he didn't look at her.

"You could have been marrying Miss Deep South back there."

He laughed. "Not my type."

"Who is then?" Okay, maybe the alcohol had loosened her lips just an itty bitty bit. She was conservative in everything she said—journalism had taught her words were power and could be used to uplift or destroy.

When he drew to a stop, he let her shoes drop to the ground. She looked down at them, and Lennon's thumb came under her chin, lifting her face up to his.

The air she'd had too little of back inside the reception hall had disappeared again.

He slipped his hand along her jawline and back behind her ear, threading his hand into her hair. She shivered at the roughness of his hand moving through her silky hair.

Looking into his eyes was stealing her resolve too.

43

She wanted him. It had been too many months since she'd been touched like this. Come to think of it, even before then, Jake wasn't very affectionate.

Before she knew what was in her mind, she went on tiptoe and moved in to kiss Lennon. The heated brush of their lips wasn't nearly enough. He cupped her head and angled her to deepen the kiss. Swiping his tongue through her mouth with desperate passes that spoke of how much he wanted her too, even if she hadn't felt the massive bulge at the front of his jeans.

She went for his shirt buttons. He found her dress zipper. In seconds, his warm hands were moving over the flesh of her spine, and she tore his shirt off his shoulders and then ripped the T-shirt out of his waistband to get her hands on what she suspected were washboard abs.

The man knew how to leave a woman wet and wanting.

She went still. His mouth continued to work along her neck to her collarbones.

"Wait. Lennon, stop."

He lifted his head immediately, eyes clear. He was completely sober. Not surprising. A big man like him could easily handle a couple whiskeys.

Knowing he was lucid and wanted her this bad... it tugged an invisible string connected to her pussy.

She pressed her hands against his hard chest. Damn, it was much harder than she'd even thought.

"Lennon, I said no strings. I can't."

"We don't need strings to enjoy each other."

She looked up into his eyes. "I'm not that kind of girl."

He searched her eyes for a moment before nodding. Slowly, he zipped her dress again and stepped back. His chest rose and fell as if he was breathing too fast. She was too.

"I think it's time to go," she said.

"I'll drive."

She nodded. He bent to swipe up his abandoned dress shirt—his poor momma would be shocked at the wrinkles put there—and then slung it over his shoulder. He grabbed her shoes too.

"Lennon..." she began.

He gave her the same smile he had every time before this, without an ounce of tension. "I had a good time with you, Edie."

Her shoulders relaxed. The day had been a whirlwind for sure, with highs and lows, moments of worry that she was making all the stupidest decisions. But in the end, Lennon was a decent man and wasn't demanding sex in payment for coming.

He held out a hand, and she took it. Together, they walked back up the slope to the parking lot. There, she stopped and he handed her the shoes, steadying her with a hand on her elbow while she put them on.

At her car, he stopped. "Sure you wanna go? You didn't get a chance at catching the bouquet."

She chuckled. "I'm not really in the market for marriage anyway. I'll take a pass."

He opened the door for her, and she got into the passenger's seat. When he got behind the wheel, he turned to her. "I know you've said you're not into dating. But I like you, Edie, and I'd like to see you again."

She hesitated, unsure what to say.

He placed a hand over hers. "Call me if you ever need a wedding date."

Shooting her a grin, he started the car. They didn't make it halfway to the road before he was staring at her thighs again.

How easy it would be to give herself to this deliciously hot man, even just one time. But she wasn't lying when she said she wasn't that girl. She believed in monogamy—and her feelings got too entangled the minute she got naked with a man. She didn't want to be distracted by thinking of Lennon for weeks after their intimate moment because her stupid heart couldn't let things go.

She had goals. Not only with *Notable News*, either. Until today when the senator didn't make an appearance, she hadn't realized what she wanted out of seeing him. Now she did.

She wanted for Bradley Arthur to look at her and know what he had missed out on all these years. It was time to figure out another way to contact him. Maybe if she offered to do an article on him, she could kill two birds with one stone.

Lennon interrupted her thoughts when he reached across the console and settled a hand on hers. "No worries between us, okay? I had a good time, and it was unexpected. I'd just come from the cemetery and wasn't thinking of life being that fun. You showed me a good time, and I'm grateful."

Her gaze shot to his face. His mouth was solemn, and for the first time she saw how serious this man could be. In fact, the lines around his mouth and the corners of his eyes weren't all from smiling, as she'd originally guessed.

"Who were you visiting, if you don't mind me asking?"

"A buddy I worked with. Lost his life to a criminal."

"I'm sorry to hear that." She turned her hand up, and meshing their fingers felt like the most natural thing in the world.

"Thanks. I was headed home, back to another buddy."

"Oh?"

"My dog. Ranger." He smiled.

She found herself smiling too, some of her stress falling away again in common talk, allowing her to forget about her reason for going to the reception in the first place.

47

* * * * *

"Man, my love life's in the shitter." Lennon's fellow Ranger Ops teammate Jess had a tendency toward the dramatic, but this time Lennon was pretty sure he was right. He love life *was* in the shitter.

He and their other buddy Cavanagh, or Cav, leaned over Jess's shoulder to stare at his phone, where a break-up text stared back at them.

Lennon clapped a hand on Jess's shoulder. "Tough break, man."

"What is wrong with women? I think I'm a pretty good guy. I take them out for dates and buy them flowers and shit. I take the time to text these chicks, and still they all dump me. Why is that?" Jess stuffed his phone in his pocket.

"You know if you didn't break the rules and have your phone on you that you never would have read that text till you got home," Cav said.

"Don't I have enough regrets without you shoving it down my throat, man?" Jess shot him a disgusted look. Even with all the black and green face paint coating his face, Jess's eyes were expressive enough to show Cav how much he didn't appreciate the observation.

"Jess, I'm kicking your ass when we get back to the city. Guys, get into position." The order came from their leader, Nash Sullivan, or Sully as they called him, into their comms devices in their ears.

"Our fearsome leader speaks," Lennon said.

"Your fearsome leader is gonna show you how fearsome he is if you assholes don't focus. We've got tracks to find and some fugitives to recover. You three get your shit together and meet up with Linc."

Lennon looked at Jess, who jerked his head to the right. Lennon and Cav fell into step behind him, each turning now and then to watch their six.

"Seriously, why would Amanda break up with me? I did everything right," Jess continued.

"That's the problem," Cav said. "You gotta treat her like shit. Girls eat that shit up."

"Why the hell would they want to be treated like shit?"

"Beats me, but I've seen it plenty. They leave good guys to chase after ones who don't give a crap about them, and pretty soon they're tied up in an awful marriage, at home doing loads of laundry for four kids while their man is having an affair at the office. And it all starts with them being treated like shit."

"That doesn't make sense." Jess swung his head right and left, keeping close vigil on the surrounding area. They'd been told the fugitives had been seen on state lines only half an hour before. They couldn't be far.

Lennon reached out and touched a leaf that was turned upside down, the bottom paler green compared to the others on the branch. "Went through here. Keep your eyes peeled."

His twin Linc stepped silently into line with them, weapon at the ready. "You guys got this women stuff all wrong. They don't want to be treated like shit. They want to be treated like a queen—just by the right man."

Jess heaved a sigh. "Think I'll turn gay instead of tryin' to figure all this shit out."

They all looked at Cav.

"Don't look at me! I'm so straight my boner's got a little black book of its own. And Jess, you couldn't go gay if you wanted. I've seen you in action, my friend."

For several minutes, Lennon listened to the quiet banter, no more than whispers between the men, as they moved in a swath across the forest in search of the fugitives.

The ops team didn't even know exactly what the guys had done, only that they'd escaped after arrest and had been hunted in three counties for a week without much ground gained until recently, when a man on an ATV had spotted them in the woods near his home. Rather than rely on the state police to recover the men, Ranger Ops had been sent.

Guess the government was tired of fucking around and sent the best of the best to end this. A week of manpower had been wasted so far, and Lennon and his team would handle it in an hour tops.

Should be easy, since the men had been living rough for a week. Not having food or access to a shower was enough to make any man desperate.

He cocked his head, and so did Linc. "Hear that?" he asked.

Linc sliced a glance at him, his nod probably imperceptible to anyone but Lennon—they had that twin bond thing going on more often than not.

Lennon slowed, his footfalls soundless on the leafy underbrush they walked through.

"Knight Ops on our nine." Sully's voice filled their ears.

Lennon wasn't going to blame that noise he'd heard on the Knight Ops team from Louisiana getting into position as backup. He concentrated on his surroundings, throwing out his senses.

Linc's head snapped around.

"Yep, heard it too," Lennon grated out. He lifted his weapon and peered through the scope. Darkness was rapidly falling, especially deep in this thick growth of woods, but his night vision scope gave him all he needed.

"Got one on the ground. Shit!" Lennon called out.

The guy jumped up and took off.

"Got him between us. Lennon, take your team and sweep around the side to avoid friendly fire!" Sully's order wasn't completely out of his mouth before Lennon was on the run. He, Linc, Cav and Jess circled fast, leaping over felled trees and sticks that might trip them.

Lennon threw a look to his side and spotted the swaying of ferns. "On the ground again. Or is that the other son of a bitch?"

"We're moving in." That came from Knight Ops.

"What are you assholes doin' on our turf, anyway?" The teasing question came from Shaw, another Ranger Ops team member and second in command.

"Who the hell knows? We get a call, we come. Seems you Rangers don't know what the hell you're doin' and OFFSUS thinks you require backup."

Lennon raised a hand to halt his team's forward progression. The flash of gunfire had them all crouching into position. "Get ready to rain hell on these fuckers," he called out, and shots shattered the quiet around them.

Doing his duty to his country and team wasn't something Lennon had to think twice about—he acted out of instinct. Actually, he rarely questioned his own decisions, but he couldn't lie about where he'd gone wrong with one pretty little blonde.

Maybe he'd gone too fast with her at the wedding. He understood that—things had heated up fast. But when they'd parted ways, she had leaned in and kissed him on lips, then thanked him for being her date. He asked if he could see her again, and she had only given a noncommittal, "We'll see."

That wasn't something that happened very often with Lennon. In fact, the only time he'd been turned down was in the ninth grade, when a girl thought he was his twin brother making a pass at her.

Lennon identified his target and took the shot. The man's forward momentum sent him pitching headfirst, where he crumpled.

An explosion of shots rang out as their second fugitive held nothing back and kept the trigger pinned beneath his finger. He was cornered and had nothing to lose.

"Drop your weapon!" Lennon bellowed.

"You'll have to kill me!" the man screamed in return.

Another spray of bullets peppered the forest, and Lennon pressed himself low in the dirt.

"Shaw, take his ass out." Sully gave the order, and one more shot was fired. All went quiet.

Lennon picked himself up off the ground with extreme caution. There were only two threats, but he never took chances.

After the solemn work of recovering the bodies, talk slowly resumed to Jess getting dumped. Then to Cav's latest score with his next door neighbor.

"Is she even legal?" Jess shot out.

"Yes. She's nineteen."

"Jesus. I don't know why you like 'em so young."

"Because they're stupid enough to think he's a hero," Lennon said with a grin.

"I am a goddamn hero—aren't we all?" Cav's grin flashed white in his dark face paint.

"Yeah, but some of us are more humble." Lennon started pulling gear off his body and stowing it in the back of the Ranger Ops SUV.

"I think it's called not getting any, Lennon."

Lennon could tell them about getting picked up at a gas pump by a beautiful and enticing woman, but he kept his mouth shut.

It wasn't until after he'd gotten into the SUV that he realized how odd that was for him. He wasn't one to kiss and tell, but he didn't hold back when he met someone he liked. Except Edie was different.

Linc climbed in next to him, and the doors all slammed shut. The vehicle rolled out, and Lennon's mind sank deep into thoughts of that wedding reception and touching Edie in all the right places. Her buttons had been pushed without a doubt, but she had put a stop to going further.

Then avoided him.

He'd texted her once since the wedding just to say hi and received no answer. He probably should call it quits and give up, but as soon as he got back home, he planned to give it one more go and call her.

From the front seat, Sully's phone buzzed.

Shit. It could only mean one thing.

54

Their leader took the call and then the tires squealed as he whipped the SUV around and turned it back toward the border.

"What the fuck's going on?" Linc asked.

"Fuuuck. I wasn't in the mood for more tonight," Shaw said. "I was up all night with the baby."

"Well, get comfy, guys. We've got a compound to rush."

"Particulars?" Shaw asked.

"Hostages and a man in a suicide vest."

They all groaned.

"I brought the grenades," Jess said from the back seat.

An hour later, instead of calling Edie, Lennon was blasting through a metal door, sweeping the area and coming out with one of the hostages.

He dumped her on the ground as gently as he could before running back in for the next while his men held off the asshole with enough explosives strapped to himself to become the first man on Mars.

As Lennon grabbed the second victim and ran with him, he was looking into the darkness lighting up with grenades his team launched at the building. But deep in his mind, what he saw was Edie's sweet face and the look in her eyes after he'd kissed her.

It was a hell of a long night, but there was still time to make a phone call.

Chapter Three

Edie pushed away from the computer desk and walked over to look out the office window, down on the streets of Austin. The *Notable News* office was in a building that was high enough she could make out pedestrians but not see their faces. If the senator walked by right now, she wouldn't recognize him.

Of course, he wouldn't be out walking the streets as a free man—he probably required bodyguards just to walk to his bathroom and take a piss. The reports of him being terrorized were increasing by the week.

All of this confused the hell out of her. He was her father, but she had no love for the man. However, she had set the goal to meet him at last and didn't want to see him killed by whatever terrorist group had him flagged.

Every law enforcement group in Texas was trying to uncover more about where the attacks stemmed from. The senator wanted better gun control laws— they wanted their guns. It was a simple tug-of-war that never should have gone this far.

But nobody seemed to be capable of protecting the senator or his family, which alarmed her. With all his money and connections, there must be someone who could help him.

Apparently, a package had shown up at his office the previous morning, but he was smart enough to have it assessed by the bomb unit, and sure enough, it was rigged.

He'd narrowly escaped with his life. The thing had been sitting right there on his desk. And how did something like that get put there in the first place? Her only answer was he worked with someone who delivered it, knowing what it was.

That had resulted in the senator dumping every person who worked for him—she wondered if Jake was included in that purge—and more bodyguards installed in his life. At this rate, she'd be lucky to ever meet him before he was assassinated.

She couldn't do anything to help the senator even if he asked. She could only dig around, use her expertise to research and see what she could uncover about these terrorists.

It wouldn't be some flagged group in the government systems. No, it had to be some second-amendment freak outfit, and she planned to find as many as possible. That meant breaching classified levels she had no access to as a lowly intern here in *Notable News*.

But Hallie had access. It was time to pay her friend another visit.

Behind Edie, the click-clack of other peons in cubicles just like hers here at the news office filled the space. She turned from the window and returned to her desk. After working another couple hours, a familiar voice had her popping her head around the wall for a peek.

Jake stood there talking to Edie's boss.

Crap — if he was working here now, it would be damn difficult to ignore him, especially when the journalism team worked so closely and held daily meetings.

"Ken will see you now," her boss said to Jake and led him past all the cubicles in the big open room to the enclosed office where the president and editor-in-chief sat in a glass-walled office overlooking Austin.

Edie's mind worked over what Jake could be doing here. Her musings that the senator had fired him along with the rest of his staff could mean Jake was here to give a statement to *Notable News* on yesterday's attempt on Senator Arthur's life.

The only thing she could do was insinuate herself into that office and listen to what was being said.

She jumped up and grabbed her notes on the topic. When she reached the editor's door, she paused to draw a deep breath before knocking. Either he'd be ticked at her for butting in or welcome her thoughts on the matter.

She rapped on the door.

The director of sales and marketing opened it for her. He looked down at her in surprise. "Miss Howard, we're in a meeting."

"I'm sorry to interrupt," she said at once. "It's just that I uncovered something that might interest—" She broke off and looked past the director to Jake, feigning surprise to see him here. "Jake."

"Edie."

"What is it that's so important, Edie?" Ken Roberts, president and editor, was not as formidable as many considered him, and Edie wasn't afraid of anybody, even one who wore Armani.

She stepped past the men gathered in the office and up to Roberts' desk. Holding out the notes she'd taken, she watched his face as he scanned the information.

His head snapped up. "Where did you find this?"

"Just took a little digging."

"More than a little. Nobody else has ever connected these dots. Good work—and keep flipping over rocks. With a nose like yours, you're likely to find more like this. Not only is it great news but could help a certain public figure."

Jake's head jerked around toward her.

"Leave this to me and return to your research, Edie," Roberts said.

She nodded. "Yes, sir. May I ask for more clearances, Mr. Roberts? I believe I would be able to get further in my search."

"Yes, give her a level B access, Gray," he said to the director.

Level B wasn't nearly enough. Hallie had way more than that, and she was an independent journalist. Edie knew she was lucky as an intern, and the lowest on the totem pole, to get *any* access here. If she wanted more information on the groups she'd listed in her notes, she would need to talk to her friend.

Plus, Jake wasn't about to openly discuss the senator with her present. She'd been a bit rash in thinking she might overhear something.

But chances untaken are lost.

She thanked her superiors and nodded to Jake before leaving the office. When she returned to her cubicle, she stared at the second set of notes she'd made, listing groups that had provided campaign funds to Senator Arthur. Below that, a series of lines connecting other names of people associated with those groups.

She hadn't delivered this set of notes to her editor. This was for herself, at least for now.

One name on that web in particular had been a stretch of the imagination, but looking at it now, she knew it might be the closest anybody had come to finding out who was attacking Senator Arthur and his family.

The man had ties to both the organization who'd donated to the senator's campaign and another group known for playing dirty, just barely remaining legal on the books and investigated more than once by the government. A look beyond that had given Edie the glimmer of light at the end of a long, dark tunnel.

George Breckham was the pivot person in both groups. On the wings, yes, but still a name that popped up in affiliation. And Breckham was a powerful New Yorker with enough money and connections to get what he wanted.

Unfortunately for him, Edie also prided herself on ancestral research, and she'd uncovered mafia ties in the 1940s and 50s. In the 60s, all of Breckham's family had cleaned up their act, and she had lost the trail.

But she knew that just because a worm presented himself as something better on the surface didn't mean he wasn't still just a worm when he went underground. With luck, Hallie would have access to the records Edie needed to discover if Breckham was still involved in the mafia, and if so, were they backing any rebel groups?

She shot off a text to Hallie, asking if she could help her. Then after work, she set off for the country roads she was becoming more and more familiar with.

* * * * *

When Hallie opened the door for Edie, she leaned in to kiss her cheek. She stepped inside and set down her weekender bag, turning to her friend. They hugged, and Hallie smiled.

61

"I'm so glad to see you, even if it's because you need to use me for my clearances," Hallie joked.

Edie wrinkled her nose. "You make me sound ungrateful. I am sorry, though. I'm happy to see you."

"If you just worked for me at the e-zine, you could have these clearances yourself, you know. But I won't ask a third time—I know you've got your eyes set on that office at *Notable News*. Come in and have a glass of wine at least. You had a long drive—and I might make you help me clean out the chicken coop later as repayment."

They shared a laugh.

She followed Hallie to the kitchen, where she poured two glasses of Zinfandel and they leaned against the counters to sip and talk.

"I saw Jake at the office," Edie said.

She arched a brow. "What was he doing there?"

"He had a meeting with the editor and director. My guess is it's got something to do with the senator."

"You never told me how the wedding reception went."

"Well... I didn't tell you because it's too much to text or say over the phone."

"Oooh, spill it, girl." Hallie set aside her glass and leaned in.

"I might have run into a guy you know and took him to the reception as my date."

Her eyes widened. "Lennon."

"How did you know that?"

"Because I ran into him weeks ago, and all he did was ask about you."

A warm shiver took hold of her.

"How do you fall into these perfect scenarios, Edie? Do you have any idea how many women want Lennon and never get a chance at him?"

"He was great at the reception, and we had a wonderful time despite the fact it was my ex getting married."

"Why *did* you go, anyhow? Just to rub it in Jake's face?"

She chewed her lip. Should she finally confide her secret that she was the illegitimate daughter of Senator Arthur and had hoped to finally meet him in the flesh?

She picked up her glass and raised it to her lips. After taking a sip, she nodded. "I think Jake, his bride and at least a hundred of his women guests were impressed with the hot guy on my arm too."

Hallie laughed. "If you're taking a revenge date, Lennon is top choice. I'll have to remember that."

They shared a chuckle and another glass of wine. Then they hit the research long into the night. For anybody else, a night of work staring at computer screens was the opposite of a fun girls' night, but for Edie and her friend, it was bonding.

When the text message came in around one in the morning, Edie blinked at the words.

Need another wedding date? I'm up for seeing you again.

She smiled.

"Is that Lennon?"

She stared at Hallie. "Why would you think it's Lennon?"

"Because you got a text at one in the morning and you're smiling at it. It could only be the hottest guy around, and that's Lennon. Or his brother Linc."

She nodded. "It is Lennon."

"Is he in the area? Are you two going to hook up?"

"No, we're not." She shook her head. She was here to work, and he hadn't said a word about being in their neck of the woods. Though if a couple wanted to be alone, there were plenty of farm roads. Suddenly, she pictured them in the bed of his truck... limbs entangled, their mouths moving together.

Their bodies moving together.

She rubbed her grainy eyes. "I'm going to get some sleep. You should too."

Hallie gave her a look. "Okay, but don't wait too long to answer that text. It's not every day a girl gets a chance at one of the Reed brothers."

She turned back to the computer screen, prepared to turn it off, when a new report popped up. Her jaw dropped.

"Oh my God, Hallie."

"What is it?" She scooted around the coffee table to look at Edie's laptop. "Wait—the senator's holding a rally?"

"It's a speech." She was stunned at how bold her biological father was. In the face of known terrorist threats, he was putting himself out there in public because he believed in speaking out about his cause.

"It will become a rally. Imagine all the press and people who will be there to oppose him, Edie."

"It's tomorrow. Crap—I'm going to have to leave now, Hallie. I'm sorry."

"I'll help you pack your car. I know when you get on the trail of a story, there's no stopping you."

* * * * *

"Here's what we got, guys." Sully hit a button and brought up an image on the big-screen. The Ranger Ops gathered around the table all groaned.

"Not that shit again. Why isn't this senator getting better protection?" Lennon said.

"We've rescued him a couple times already," Jess added.

"Yeah, well, he's giving a speech in Austin, but it's going to turn ugly with picketers and guys with flags spouting off about keeping their guns. We don't need to care about whether or not we support the senator, but we have to be on the alert. If we get that

65

call to go in, we have to be on the ready." Sully switched off the screen, and it went black.

"So we're heading to Austin." Lennon's statement had Sully nodding.

"We leave now. We've got a hotel."

"I hope that means room service," Cav said.

"It means get your shit loaded up, because we roll out in ten." Sully walked out of the conference room.

Everyone stared after him.

"What crawled up his ass?" Jess asked.

"Think he's just tired. Or sick of protecting dumbass senators." Shaw rubbed at his face, but he couldn't erase the tired lines there. His new baby was keeping him and his wife Atalee up all hours of the day and night. It seemed the little bundle of joy had become a little bundle of insomnia.

Lennon was damn glad he wasn't trying to juggle a family life and the Ranger Ops too—it was difficult enough trying to find time to date.

Of course, it would be easier if the girl he actually wanted to date would reply to his texts. But he'd only sent the latest message a little while ago, and it was the middle of the night. She was most likely asleep, not waiting up for texts.

He pushed away from the table. "I'm dragging. I hope this rally doesn't get out of control and we can catch some sleep at the hotel, at least."

Linc clasped his shoulder and squeezed. "You know it's gonna get out of control. But the speech is scheduled for the afternoon. So you can grab a few hours of shuteye before we get called in."

"Why can't this shit all go down on the weekdays?" Lennon and Linc moved to the conference room door and down the hall of their base office, toward the lockers that held all their gear, which they'd just stowed away after their back-to-back duties.

"Yeah, Nealy and I were planning to visit Momma this weekend. You heard from her lately?" Linc threw a glance at him.

"Just texts. It will be good for you two to visit her. I wish she'd move closer to us." Lennon opened his locker and started pulling out gear.

"Not likely, so we'll just need to keep making time to visit. She was good last time you went, though, right?"

"Yes, she was great. We had a nice weekend."

"Good. I feel guilty Nealy and I haven't been there for a couple months."

"Pretty damn hard when we're dealing with this shit." Lennon reached for his bulletproof vest.

"It's difficult enough making time for Nealy. Be glad you don't have a woman in your life, Lennon. It only gets harder." Linc had all his gear ready and shut his locker with a *clang*.

Lennon stared at his twin's back as he walked away. While he knew he wasn't really prepared to have the life some of his teammates did with wives and children, he couldn't stop thinking about seeing Edie again.

He hoped she texted back.

* * * * *

"Limiting gun violence begins with..."

Edie was squeezed from all sides by the crowd, and it was making it damn difficult to listen to the senator on stage when she had a woman's elbow jammed into her side.

She twisted away and shot the woman a dirty look before concentrating on the podium where Senator Arthur stood.

He was those two D words—dashing and debonair. Dressed in a fine charcoal gray suit with a dark purple tie, he looked as though he'd just stepped off the pages of *GQ*. Against his white shirt, his tanned skin glowed. He might have recently taken a trip to his second home in Colorado.

Edie's gaze traveled upward. Strong features covered that face she only saw on TV. A straight nose, full lips, and wide blue eyes. Looking at Senator Arthur was like blurring the lines of her own reflection and adding masculine details.

She had her own blonde hair pulled back into a severe ponytail and her glasses on to conceal the color of her eyes—exactly like the senator's.

That elbow was back in her ribs. She pushed against the woman's arm to remove it, which earned her a dirty look from the woman. If it wasn't wall-to-wall people, Edie would move.

This was also the best view of Senator Arthur, and if that meant standing around with a sharp elbow jabbing her ribs, she'd do it.

"The second amendment says..."

"Asshole!" someone screamed out.

The shout came from deep in the crowd, and it roused several others to repeat it.

"Asshole!"

"Shut up, you traitor asshole!"

Edie stared at the senator's face and saw no change in his expression. He continued to speak, giving his spiel on increasing restrictions on weapons while still retaining the right to bear arms. In her opinion, and she was no politician, that was Senator Arthur's biggest mistake.

He was trying to sit on both sides of the fence, keep everybody happy. Keep those voters in his pocket.

But in this world, he couldn't please everyone, and that caused him worse results at the voting polls. He was also taking a huge risk in being in the public eye. Even with the tight security in the arena, she didn't trust that somebody hadn't gotten a weapon through.

The crowd grew inflamed, jostling her side to side. She pitched forward and caught herself before she fell to her knees. She'd never get up if she hit the ground, and the way the crowd was acting, she'd probably be trampled.

"You've listened to me enough for one afternoon. I'd like to hear from you. Who's willing to come up here and argue for or against me today?"

Edie's heart beat hard. This was her chance. She knew the senator's thoughts on the topic inside and out. With her background, Edie had written plenty on both sides of the biggest argument in the country in this decade. And she had plenty to say.

She stared at the man at the podium. If she got onstage, it would be the closest she'd ever stood to her father.

She should not get up there with the senator. But he might be dead soon from some violent act or other, and she'd never get the chance to show him the kind of person she was.

She lunged through an opening in the crowd and somehow, miraculously, came up against the stage. She scrambled up, and the senator turned to look at her.

"Here's one eager young woman." As soon as his gaze lit on her, she swore he paled under his tan.

He recognizes me.

Too late to go back now, he waved for her to step forward.

She stared out over the massive crowd gathered to hear him speak — and now it was her turn to speak.

She was excellent at public speaking, and she'd often believed it an inherited trait.

"Thank you, Senator Arthur," she said smoothly as she stepped toward him.

He held out a hand, but she saw the hesitation in his eyes. A perverse part of her who'd always longed to be one of his claimed offspring felt like poking *him* in the ribs. *How's it feel to finally look your daughter in the eyes, eh, Daddy?*

She clasped his hand and studied his face up close. "Nice to meet you."

"Thank you for coming today." His throat sounded closed off, the words strangled.

She nodded and stepped past him, up to the podium, aware of how much taller he was when she had to adjust the microphone. She was aware of bodyguards standing close.

"Go home, Senator!" someone bellowed, and a chorus of boos followed.

Edie waited a long minute for the din to die down, and then she began speaking. With no real speech in mind, she simply spoke from the heart. What it came down to, in her eyes, was that something needed to change in their country, and they all needed to listen to everybody who had something to say on the subject in order to form a good opinion and choose the right people for office. Even if it wasn't Senator Arthur.

She looked across the stage to her father, standing there looking suddenly older. Hunched and beaten down by the heckling of the crowd.

Or maybe beaten down by the fact he was listening to his daughter's voice for the very first time.

After she relinquished the podium to another speaker, Edie scrambled back through the crowd and made her way to the parking garage.

When she hit the unlock button and reached for the door handle, a car pulled up behind and hemmed her in.

The back window rolled down, and she was staring at her father.

"Get in," he said and then rolled up the window.

Heart pounding, she weighed her options. She could run away and refuse to speak to him, but she had hoped for this moment.

Her footsteps sounded incredibly loud in the parking garage — or maybe that was her heart pounding in her ears.

She reached for the door handle, but the door pushed open from the inside. She slid in.

"Close the door." His blue eyes burned into hers. "Nate," he said to the driver.

The car rolled smoothly through the dim garage.

"You took a huge risk today in coming here, Eden."

"Edie. I go by Edie."

His gaze latched onto her face, and she couldn't tell by his scowl if he didn't like her nickname or didn't like to be corrected or interrupted.

"Edie, you compromised us both. In a big way."

"I won't be chastised for speaking out on my opinions, which helped you, by the way."

"You're a smart girl—I've heard that enough from your mother."

They kept in touch? She'd always assumed there was some secret bank account where money was deposited for Edie's wellbeing and nothing more.

"You know I've spent the last year and a half fighting to keep myself and my family safe. And after you stepped on that stage with me, and everybody in that arena and every reporter in the country snapped photos of us together, you've just added another target to the terrorists' list."

She swallowed.

His gaze traveled over her pale hair and latched onto her blue eyes. She felt like she was looking into a mirror.

"Eden—Edie," he corrected himself in a heated tone, "you've got to get out of the spotlight now. Lay low."

"Lay low. What does that mean?"

"It means that whatever you've been doing for years, you have to do differently. If you take the six-thirty bus, you have to take another at a different

73

time. These people will find you. No, they will *hunt* you, Edie."

She blinked at him. "I know they've been targeting you and your... family." The word was a choked and hollow sound. "But—"

"But you've made the entire nation aware of our ties!" He gripped her hand.

She stared at their fingers, her face hot with emotion and the embarrassment that she hadn't given enough thought to the entire situation before making the snap decision to get onstage.

A car in front of them and one behind kept them protected—that alone jolted her to awareness. He was a guarded man, and he was sitting here telling her she had to hide.

He released her hand and reached into his jacket, pulling out a long wallet. He opened it and removed a stack of cash. "Keep low. Change your lifestyle. Take this to get you by until you find another job—not in journalism either—but I suggest leaving no paper trail. Get something that pays under the table."

She wasn't aware they had circled the garage and arrived back at her car until they stopped.

Senator Arthur shoved the cash into her hand. "I can't help you after this, Edie. I can't help any of my family. I wish you hadn't put yourself in danger. You're the last person I can't protect."

With that, he reached across her and opened the door.

She got out of the car and watched him drive away, the red taillights blurred in her vision as the tears came.

*****

"We're in the clear. The senator left right after his speech and didn't return. The police are handling the mob of people leaving the arena, but it looks like we won't be needed this afternoon, boys."

Sully's news had a cheer going up. Linc and Shaw pushed to their feet. "Good. We're heading back."

Jess and Cav exchanged a look. "Think we might stay here and enjoy the hot tub downstairs, if nobody cares," Cav drawled.

"You just saw those coeds down in the lobby," Lennon said with a grin.

"You only live one life. Might as well enjoy myself." Cav planted a big foot on the floor and pushed up to his full height. He topped Lennon by a good inch. "You stayin' to keep us company, Lennon?"

"Nah, I think I'll go back with the others. My dog's waitin' for me at home."

"Or the dog sitter is..." Jess's comment had several of the guys tossing out their two cents about her services, but Lennon waved them all away.

They left Jess and Cav to make their own way back home, and the trip passed quickly. When Lennon arrived at his house, he saw Deanna outside with Ranger on a leash, just returning from their afternoon walk.

He got out of his truck and threw her a grin as Ranger almost yanked her arm out of the socket trying to reach Lennon. He crouched to meet the dog, who pulled free. The dog attacked him with kisses, and Lennon rubbed his big square head and talked to him.

Deanna walked up hesitantly. "He's really missed you this time."

He stood and caught the end of the leash so Ranger didn't take off after a rabbit or squirrel. "Thanks for stayin' longer with him."

"About that, Lennon..." She was a student who'd grown up in this neighborhood, and she was a blessing for Lennon and Ranger. But she looked at him with a worried expression.

He held his breath.

"I got another job. Something with better hours. I've loved watching Ranger while you're gone, and I'll miss him so much, but I'd like some kind of a personal life, and I can't have that working for you."

Hell, now what?

He understood. It just sucked. And he had all of five minutes to find a replacement, because he couldn't risk being called out with nobody lined up to take care of Ranger.

If he couldn't care for a dog, how could he even think about a long-term relationship, or what was more, kids?

"I'm sorry to hear that, Deanna, but I get it. You've been excellent for Ranger, and we both appreciate it so much. Come inside and I'll pay what I owe you."

After he gave her some cash and a hefty tip, he and Ranger were left staring at each other.

Even though Ranger already had his walk, he was always up for another. Lennon changed his clothes and shoes and then grabbed the leash again.

Ranger jumped around in excitement, only standing still long enough for Lennon to hook him up. "Let's go, boy. We'll find you a new dog sitter when we get back."

What Lennon needed was a run to clear his head and get rid of some of his pent-up frustration about his life. He loved his job, didn't want to give it up. But the past few days... he was thinking about having more.

That might have something to do with Edie.

Or it might be his desire not to exit this world without having someone who loved him the way his buddy Adam had done. Cav was right—life was short. While Lennon didn't want to flirt with young coeds, he knew he wouldn't have many chances at grabbing happiness.

The last time he'd been happy was with Edie. Talking to her, laughing with her. They had managed to have fun at her ex's wedding, and that told Lennon that they could enjoy themselves anywhere.

Wasn't that what it was like to have a life partner?

After a long jog with Ranger, Lennon returned home and got them both drinks. While Ranger slurped away, he checked his phone. No reply from Edie.

She must really not be into him.

No, he didn't buy that. She had responded with much enthusiasm to his advances. It had crossed his mind that she could still be hung up on her ex, but she hadn't given the guy a second glance at his reception. She had, however, sent quite a few looks toward the door as if waiting for someone to walk in.

He couldn't shake the connection he'd felt for her. He had to give it one more shot before moving on. He kept saying that—one more shot. When was he going to give up?

He sent off another text.

Of all your beautiful curves, your smile is my favorite one. Go out with me.

A bit on the cheesy side, but he was shooting for lighthearted, something to put that smile he loved on her face.

Now he just had to sit back and hope it worked. In the meantime, he would search for a new dog sitter.

* * * * *

"What are you doing here?" Edie opened her apartment door to a surprise visit from Hallie. She hadn't called ahead, just shown up on the security camera when she buzzed in to Edie's apartment building.

She hurriedly shut the door behind Hallie and stared at her friend.

"I have something for you." Hallie placed a hand over the messenger bag slung across her body.

"Couldn't you have sent it?"

"Not this." She opened the bag and pulled out a sheaf of papers. On the top was the photo of Edie onstage with Senator Arthur.

She sucked in a breath.

"I've been patient with your explorations into the senator's life, Edie. I realize it's a huge story and that it would help push you out of the internship into a permanent position at *Notable News*. But this..." She tapped the photo showing them together, her pale hair a beacon to the public that she had a familial tie to the politician.

Edie swallowed hard. "Come in." She twisted the door lock just in case. While she wasn't certain what the senator had said to her — lay low — wasn't an overreaction on his part, she felt more comfortable not taking chances.

She went into the living room and sank to the couch, staring into space.

Hallie dropped beside her. "What is going on, Edie? I'm your closest friend — don't you trust me?"

"I do," she said at once. "It's just that... nobody knows."

"Knows what?" Hallie searched her face for answers.

A heartbeat passed. "That Senator Arthur is my father. I'm the product of his extramarital affair with my mother, who was reporting his story from the start of his career. But now it seems like everybody knows."

Hallie pushed out a breath. "My God, Edie. I saw this photo and had to ask, but I didn't think I would be right."

She reached for the photo and wished she had never gotten up on that stage.

She shook herself and laid the photo on the rustic coffee table in front of her.

"Maybe people won't draw conclusions."

"You did," Edie said flatly.

"Only because I know how involved you are in finding out more about the senator. Is that why you stayed so long with Jake?"

She dropped her gaze to her knotted hands. She nodded. "I think it might be."

"Oh, Edie." Hallie's voice echoed the despair she felt.

Should she share what had happened after the rally—that the senator had followed her to the garage, asked her to get in and then scared the hell out of her with what he had to say to her?

He didn't even know the name I go by.

It was a silly thing to distract her, but her mind kept returning to the fact that he had called her Eden. Nobody called her that except people who didn't know her.

Of course he didn't know her—he'd never tried to.

Despite hating him for that, she still wanted to help him by uncovering more about the tie to Breckham she'd found the other day. She couldn't shake the idea that there was a link.

"Edie, I found something else."

She jerked her gaze up to her friend's. "What is it?" Her voice came out weak.

"I got this from a friend of a friend. He knows a lot of insider information."

"I'm listening," Edie prompted.

"There's rumor of an informant. On Senator Arthur. Somebody who works for him on the inside."

"I knew it." She snatched up the picture again but didn't really see the faces that resembled each other so much. "Do you have a name?"

Hallie shook her head. "Like I said, it's a rumor."

"But you don't just follow rumors, Hallie. You have cold, hard facts."

"Yes, and as soon as I have a contact, I will get it to you. I thought you also might be able to do something with this."

"Give me what you have."

Hallie handed her the sheaf of papers, and Edie sat back to skim a few pages before lowering the stack to her lap.

She let out a sigh. "I thought I might read something about Jake. I'm glad I was wrong, because I never thought he was crooked, just ambitious."

"No, I don't think it's Jake," Hallie said.

Edie nodded. "Thank you for driving all that way to bring me this, Hallie. You're the best friend."

"I wish I could do more to help you."

"Just keep being there for me, okay? You know I love you."

"Love you too, sister from another mister."

They laughed.

"You really are from another mister, aren't you? All right, I have a long drive back and a deadline to meet. The e-zine goes out day after tomorrow. I don't suppose you'll come with me as my second set of eyes?"

Edie shook her head.

"I already knew that. It's okay."

Long after Hallie left for home, Edie sat there staring into space. Occasionally, she picked up the photo and searched her own face and then Senator Arthur's. To her, the resemblance was uncanny. Who else would see it? His family who knew nothing about her, reporters... terrorist groups?

She had some hard choices to make, and it was all due to her stupid act at the rally. She either had to listen to the senator and change her life until this all blew over, or she would go about her life as it was and chalk up his words to overreaction.

By the time the first rays of dawn seeped through the window, she was convinced the senator had only reacted strongly to seeing her. Perhaps he'd even felt some paternal concern for her safety.

She would go about her business as usual and return to her internship on Monday morning. In the meantime, she would take the rest of her weekend to comb through all the information Hallie had provided her with.

But then she found the note, slipped under her door sometime during the night.

Stay out of sight. Don't go out.

Chapter Four

Lennon flipped through the pages of the classified ads on his computer tablet, scanning them for people looking for work as a dog sitter. At this point, even a babysitter might be willing to cross over to canine care.

He was damn lucky the Ranger Ops team hadn't been called out over the past few days, but to cover his ass, he'd spoken with his neighbor about dropping by and letting Ranger out, feeding him or even allowing him into the fenced back yard for exercise while Lennon was away.

The neighbor was in agreement, but she had also suggested Lennon give the dog up for adoption or rehome him if he didn't have time for Ranger.

Which left Lennon grinding his teeth. He loved that dog, and he'd gotten Ranger as a rescue after Adam died. It didn't take the place of his friend, but it had taken his mind off the worst.

Getting rid of Ranger wasn't an option—he needed the help.

He grabbed his phone and called Linc. His twin picked up after two rings.

"'Sup, bro?"

"I'm calling for some advice. I lost Deanna as my dog sitter."

Ranger wanted out into the fenced yard, and he opened the back door off the kitchen to set him free. He bounded out and grabbed one of the balls he'd left outside. Lennon stood at the door watching him.

"Tough break. She was reliable."

"Yeah. Know anybody who would work out for me?" Lennon asked.

"No, I don't. But I'll ask Nealy. She may know somebody. Have you checked the paper?"

"Yeah."

"Then you also saw the senator's targeted again."

"No, I haven't. I skipped the headlines and went straight to the classifieds." He turned from the door and grabbed his tablet again. When he brought up the page, he stared harder. Then he tapped the image to get a closer look.

"Son of a bitch," he said quietly as he recognized that pale hair and the curves he'd been fantasizing about for weeks.

"Sucks for the senator, but it might mean we're kept close to home in case of another big attack on him. At least we won't be sent to Mexico anytime soon."

Linc kept talking, but Lennon wasn't listening. He was skimming the article. It made no mention of Edie.

But that sure as hell was her. And the senator sure as hell shared a lot of her looks.

He used his thumb and forefinger on the screen to enlarge the image. The pixels made it blurry, but he zoomed in on the woman's face. He'd know that delicate chin and those wide eyes, even hidden behind glasses, anywhere.

"Lennon? Dinner?"

He was jarred from his thoughts, returning to his brother's conversation. "What's that?" he asked.

"Nealy asked if you'll have dinner with us tonight. She's making a roast and said there's plenty."

"Roast sounds good," he said automatically.

"Good. See ya at six."

Lennon hung up, and the dog scratched the door to get back in. He walked blindly to the door and opened it for him. Ranger ran to his water bowl. Lennon had to get in touch with Edie.

What would he even say? She hadn't answered him after the first attempts, and it was quite unlikely she would respond to his question about her tie to a politician who was always in danger.

Fuck—he didn't like this one bit.

He grabbed his phone and thumbed a text to her once again. This time, he asked if she knew anybody who'd be interested in a dog sitting position. It was the first thing that came to mind.

When he saw the little blip on the screen that she was responding to his text, his heart beat faster.

I happen to know someone.

Jesus. She'd answered.

That's great! Who?

Me.

He pressed a button to call her. She picked up immediately, and his libido did a leap at the sound of her feminine voice even as his chest tightened with worry.

"Hi there," he said. "I'm glad you answered your phone."

"Hi. I got your messages. They were cute."

He closed his eyes, envisioning her, and then opened them and looked at the article and photo still up on his tablet. "So... you need a job?"

"I'm looking for something, yes." He heard the strain in her tone loud and clear. He was trained to hear things others didn't.

"Maybe we can talk in person then." He had to see her, just to make sure she was all right. Things were too odd and coincidental for his liking. Her photo made the headlines, she looked too much like the senator's relation and now she was in need of a lowly job he had on offer?

He bit back what he really wanted to say.

"Can you meet me, Edie?" he asked instead.

A heartbeat of silence passed.

"Edie?"

"I'm here."

"Something's wrong. Where are you?"

"My apartment."

"Give me the address. I'm coming for you." His commanding tone wasn't something most people scoffed off. Edie hesitated, though. Damn, the woman was a hard ass.

"Edie."

I saw the photo and I'm making a guess at who you are and why you suddenly need a job.

"I really could use a reliable person for my dog."

"Ranger," she said.

"That's right. I'm coming by now. I just need the address."

She gave it to him, and he locked the doors and set the alarm before heading out to his truck, taking long strides. She was located only about thirty minutes from him, but he hoped the interstate wasn't blocked with traffic like it normally was. On a Sunday morning, it might be smoother cruising.

He had to get to her fast. He didn't like this one bit.

I can protect her.

How to explain all he'd avoided telling her about his line of work the other times they'd gotten together?

Edie wasn't the only one with secrets. But he had a feeling it would take some hefty explosives to shake them out of her.

Especially since it seemed she had a lot of reasons to bury them.

* * * * *

She'd believed herself safe — too far removed from the Arthur family to be afraid.

But she'd made a bad decision in going onstage at the speech.

Journalists died all the time getting stories, even when they weren't connected to politicians with hate groups threatening him.

She regretted giving Lennon her address, or even picking up the phone. She didn't want him involved. But that note slid deep in the pocket of her jeans seemed to scorch her skin.

Stay out of sight. Don't go out.

How was she supposed to function under these conditions? If she didn't go out, she couldn't run from her current life.

At least she had the bit of cash the senator had given her. A little over five hundred dollars would see her through for a while until she figured out if she could even draw on her bank account without somebody noting her activity and locating her.

As someone who knew what human beings were capable of, she finally felt what the Arthur family must have been feeling all this time — terrified and helpless.

You're the last person I can't protect. Her father's hopeless words rang through her mind, louder now that she understood what he meant.

How had all this happened in such a short time? Days ago, she was only worried about getting the best story, landing that full-time position at *Notable News*. Now, she was considering giving it all up and going off with a cowboy she'd only made out with one time with the prospect of becoming his dog sitter?

She dragged her fingers through her hair, wishing it wasn't such an unusual and prominent color. She should have dyed it before going up on that stage.

She threw a few items into a bag—jeans, tees, sensible shoes in case she did become a dog's caregiver instead of the hard-nosed journalist she had worked hard to become.

When she reached into her underwear drawer, she touched on the sexy pair she'd been wearing under the red dress at Jake's wedding. Lennon had never gotten a chance to see them. She hooked the lacy thong with a finger and dropped the panties into her bag along with her comfier cotton ones.

Then she rushed to the bathroom, grabbing any trial sizes of products she had on hand and tossing in her toothbrush too.

Back in the living room, she spotted the papers Hallie had brought. Those went into the bag as well, along with her phone charger.

She stopped and looked around her apartment. If she was bugging out of her life for a while, she needed to make some calls to those who would notice.

Her boss. Hallie. And her mother.

Her mother was overseas right now. She might not have seen the article yet, being in a different time zone.

She shot off a text to her, giving her the bare minimum of information. *I'm okay. Laying low for a while. I'll be in touch. Please don't worry. I love you.*

Then her boss. *Had a family emergency. Will be out of town for a while. Hope to see you soon.*

Lastly, Hallie.

The door buzzer sounded, alerting her that Lennon was here. Her heart raced as she looked at the security camera. Even from the overhead angle and in black and white, Lennon was big and sexy.

She ran her hand over her face. Was she really drawing him into this?

He was a good means for her to stay hidden, though. She wouldn't leave a paper trail with a paycheck for dog sitting. Her own place would still be here when she returned, the rent and all her bills paid from direct withdrawal, and she had a small savings built up.

She didn't see any choice. The universe was giving her a safe haven in Lennon.

She pressed the button to unlock the door for him.

* * * * *

God, he just wanted to scoop her up and never let go.

Lennon's initial reaction to seeing Edie again wasn't among the normal ones for him. Besides wanting to press a thumb over the skin of her brows to smooth it, he felt pretty damn betrayed that she hadn't confided in him. Which left him pissed off as well. All that heaped onto his protective urge to hide her away.

He stepped inside and immediately swept a glance around the place. It was his usual way to scope out danger, but all he saw was a homey place with lamps, mirrors, knickknacks and comfortable pillows.

He reached out to take her hand. She let him have it, and he closed his fingers around hers, feeling an electric bolt run up his arm.

"It's good to see you," he said.

She tried to smile but failed. "You too. Thanks for coming." She shot a look at the security screen near the door as if checking for someone to have followed him.

His inner protector kicked into high gear. He could be overreacting, but why take chances? He could get her out of here fast.

"Look, my dog sitter left me high and dry. I'm in a field of work where I travel often, and at a moment's notice. I don't have family nearby to watch Ranger, so I'm looking to hire someone. I can give you the spare room in my house. No strings."

She blinked up at him, eyes bluer than he remembered. Maybe it was the blue shadows beneath her eyes exaggerating the color.

"It seems an imposition to you, Lennon," she said.

"No imposition. It's convenience. Like a live-in nanny. For my dog." He hoped his light tone would earn him a smile, but her reaction was another crinkle of her brow.

"What if Ranger doesn't like me?"

"He likes everybody. Besides, he's already smelled you... on me."

Her gaze leaped to his. A flush coated her cheeks, and his insides stirred with desire.

She slanted a look at her bag, already packed not far away from where they stood. "It's a good offer, and one that's welcome right now. You see, I'm being... evicted." She gave a sad look around her apartment.

She was lying, and he knew it. He nodded anyway.

"Then you can stay with me till you get on your feet. I'll give you room and board and all the long walks you can handle with Ranger. And pay too, of course."

"Room and board's enough for now, Lennon. I'm having a streak of bad luck, but I hope it ends soon."

He studied her tense shoulders and the worried light in her eyes. "I live half an hour away. If you forgot to take anything —"

"I didn't," she said at once. "I mean... a friend is going to take over the lease and won't mind me leaving some things here until I can get on my feet." She moved to pick up her bag, but Lennon was there to remove it from her hand.

"Ready?" What he really meant was she ready for him to protect her?

She nodded and led the way out of the apartment.

He took over the lead, scanning the area for dangers as he took her out to his truck and put her inside.

This all felt way too much like one of the Ranger Ops missions to be normal protocol. His radar hadn't been blaring for nothing. Edie was acting strange because she was in danger. And by his guess, it was due to that photo of her splashed all over the country.

He wanted to tell her he'd keep her safe, that nothing would get past him.

But he had a feeling he'd be protecting himself even more. The woman was already tugging hard on his heart.

* * * * *

Edie had to start keeping track of the tall tales she was telling Lennon. Good thing she had a strong memory, because she could easily trip herself up.

She also felt horrible about it. She was no liar — the truth was her life, and she was dedicated to reporting it, even when it would hurt. Lennon was being so nice to her, and if she was honest, he was flat out coming to her rescue.

She liked him, and lying to him was no way to repay him.

When he unlocked his house by punching a security code into an alarm system, she breathed a sigh of relief. The security was welcome, especially after receiving that note under her apartment door. She'd believed her building to be one of the safest in the city, yet someone had managed to get inside and deliver that message.

Glancing up and down the street, she took note of normal houses with normal cars parked out front and pots of flowers on porches. More than one American flag flew, and one was beside Lennon's front door.

With a hand on the doorknob, he turned to look at her. "Prepare yourself."

She eyed him, heart starting that off-beat, which had started back when she'd read the note. "Okay…"

He grinned and then opened the door.

A dog blasted out, leaped at Lennon twice before dashing into the front yard and doing a circle. Then he ran back full tilt, knocking into her legs to reach his master.

Lennon said a word, and the black lab dropped to a sit, but his butt continued to wiggle with excitement.

"This is Ranger. Ranger, meet Edie." He rubbed the dog's blocky head.

"Hi, Ranger." She held out a hand for the dog to sniff. He barely took a whiff before he was leaning into her hand, demanding pets.

As stressed as she was, the action had a smile spreading across her face. She could see why there were therapy dogs now. Maybe she needed one of her own to combat fear and for bodily protection. This big, strong dog seemed capable of taking down anybody who tried to mess with her.

She rubbed Ranger's ear, and his legs went out from under him.

Lennon laughed. "You found a good spot."

"I see that."

He looked past her, his gaze sweeping the street in a way that had her wondering what kind of training he had. She'd interviewed her share of law enforcement officers, and they were often behaving the same way Lennon was. He'd told her he worked for a government agency, and now she was questioning what that was.

"Come inside," he said.

She followed him indoors. The cooler air felt good on her hot face. He set down her bag he'd insisted on carrying from the car and turned to her. Before he spoke, a scratching noise came from the back of the house.

"Ranger wants out back to do his business. Just a minute."

She watched him walk away, long legs clad in denim making her think of sneaking off to that creek with him... of how he'd touched her and how she'd wanted to touch him back.

Now she was going to stay in his house. It was too late to decide whether or not it was a good idea. She didn't have anywhere else to go.

She took the precious seconds alone to look at her surroundings. Lennon was surprisingly neat for a bachelor. The small space they'd passed through into the living area had everything in its place—shoes lined up neatly and coats hung on hooks. The living area had wooden floors in a warm chestnut tone. The only furniture was a leather sofa facing a big-screen TV. In one corner of the sofa was a crumpled pillow that looked as though he'd fallen asleep there at some point.

Beyond that, the area unfolded to what might be a dining room, but he had a desk set up with two computer monitors. She looked closer. Either he was a gamer or his work involved looking at more than one thing at a time.

He walked back in, a smile on his face belying the crinkle of his brow. Rubbing a hand over his dark brown hair, he said, "It's not much, but I hope you'll find it comfortable here."

"It's nice. Neat."

"You sound surprised." He chuckled.

"Most bachelor pads I've walked into I was met by a stench of trash and dirty dishes."

"I admit I'm not home enough to accumulate either. But I have to keep the trash out or else Ranger finds something good in the can."

She smiled.

"Come see the rest of the place." He held out a hand, and she walked forward to take it. The minute his warm, rough fingers enfolded hers, a sense of calm washed over her. He liked her—his voicemails and her times with him said as much. Maybe she was taking advantage of his feelings for her, but she didn't know what else to do right now. As soon as she discovered which way was up in her life, she'd make things right with Lennon. Until then, she was going to enjoy the safe feelings he shrouded her with.

The kitchen was surprisingly open and spacious for the size. He didn't have junk cluttering the countertops, and the only dirt was a few toast crumbs scattered in front of the toaster.

There were two big windows letting in tons of light, and a door opened onto a back yard. The wood had scratch marks from Ranger wanting out.

Lennon opened the door, and they stepped onto a small paved patio area. A single chair sat there along with a big manly grill, and dog toys were scattered through the grass.

"I bet you sit out here and just throw toys for him to fetch," she said.

"Yes. That will be your job too now." He smiled down at her, and her insides clenched. He still had hold of her hand, and he used it to draw her a step closer. "Edie, I want you to think of this as your place too. You have access to everything. Nothing's off-limits... except the grass. I like mowing the lawn."

A wide smile tipped up her lips. "A true country boy."

"I have to live here to be close to work, but I like to live the country life when I can. My momma has two acres of land — not much when you consider the size of some of those farms and ranches around her. But it was my job to cut the grass, and I guess it's stuck with me."

"Don't worry — I won't take over that duty." She wrinkled her nose.

The dog trotted back inside and went straight to his water bowl. He lapped long and loud for a minute before lifting his head with a wet smile. Lennon chuckled. "C'mon, boy. Let's show Edie her room."

She was pleased to hear she wouldn't have a permanent spot on the couch and followed him down a short hall off the kitchen.

"This is my room." He shoved open a door, revealing a king-sized bed with dark green blankets, a wooden nightstand and a lamp. All simple, masculine and more intriguing to Edie than it should be.

"This is the bathroom. I'm sorry—we have to share."

"It's a good size," she said. There was a separate tub and a glass-walled shower.

Too easily she could picture Lennon's big body behind that glass... naked, muscled and slick with water. She twisted away.

He took another few steps to a closed door. When he pushed it open, she stepped inside. The room was small, but what did she really need? A double bed stood against the wall, the mattress bare. The two windows letting in streamers of golden sunlight also were undressed.

She turned to him. "Your last dog sitter didn't live here?"

"No, she lives down the street. I've never used this room, never had a guest over."

She studied his face, but his expression didn't give away whether or not he'd had women guests who stayed with him in that king-sized bed. A hard kernel of tension hit Edie's stomach.

Lennon released her hand and walked over to a closet. He opened it and reached onto a high shelf. When he turned with a bag of brand-new bedding, he gave her a sheepish grin. "My mother gave me this bedding as a housewarming gift, but..." He set it on the mattress and waved at the pale green set. "It's not exactly my thing. Besides, I have a king-sized."

She nodded. "It's a little feminine for you."

"Yeah, Momma means well."

"Most mommas do." They shared a glance that turned into something intense enough that Edie felt suddenly overheated. She pulled her stare from his. "This will be great. I'll make the bed."

"Oh, I almost forgot." He walked to the closet once more and turned with two packs of white curtains in hand. "If you don't mind hanging these too."

"Of course not. Lennon, you've been so generous. Thank you."

"I'm the one who should be thanking you. You've saved my hide by agreeing to watch Ranger."

Speaking of Ranger, the dog had found them. He wandered into the room and jumped onto the bed. Edie let out a laugh as he curled up like he owned the room.

"Ranger, you blockhead. Get down." Lennon tugged the dog's collar, but Ranger just laid there unmoving.

"It's okay, isn't it, Ranger? You can lay here for a little while."

"He shouldn't be allowed to think this is his bed. You don't have to put up with watching a dog and then sleeping with him."

Lennon's words... sleeping with... had their gazes locking once more. That initial attraction she'd felt at the honkytonk bar, the date at the Italian restaurant and then when she'd danced in his arms at her ex's wedding reception hadn't lessened one bit. Her body was still screaming out for him to place his callused hands on her.

She dropped her gaze to his chest, but that only had her thinking of pressing him down on the bed and straddling him.

She bit back a groan and lifted her gaze to his once more. "I'll make sure to close my door so Ranger can't come in."

Suddenly, Lennon went still. His throat worked a moment before he spoke. "Edie, whatever trouble you're in, I'll do anything I can to help you."

"Like I said, it's just a streak of bad luck. I'll be on my feet in no time." *Or out of hiding.*

She had to find out what she could. Maybe he wouldn't mind her using his computer while he was out of the house. She'd have to ask.

"Well, until then, *mi casa es su casa.* Now, I don't know about you, but I'm starving. I'm pretty sure I've got steaks in the fridge that are still good. What do you say? I know you're not vegan—I saw you eat prime rib at the wedding."

She grinned. "I'm not vegan, and steak sounds delicious. I'll just make the bed and then come help you."

He reached out and caught her fingers in his hold again, pressing them lightly before letting go. After he left the room, Ranger got up to follow, leaving her to unpackage the bedding and make the bed. She was too short to reach the curtain rods without a chair, so that would have to wait. She stood back to examine her new space.

She didn't want to be here, not really. But if she had to be on the lam, at least she felt comfortable with Lennon. She had to admit, everything had fallen into place for her. The muscled man, the watchdog, a security system installed in his home and even the remote residential street where he lived gave Edie the ability to draw a deep breath again, something she hadn't since the senator's speech the other day.

She was okay here for now.

The dog's toenails clacked on the hardwood as he entered the room again. When she sat on the edge of the bed to lure him near, he took it one step further by bounding up on the mattress with her.

The scent of grilling meat wafted to her through some open kitchen window, and her stomach growled. Ranger looked at her.

"I promise I'll give you my scraps, boy. Okay?" She rubbed his side, and he flipped onto his back to present his belly. She laughed. "We're going to get along fine, aren't we?"

She had no worries about the dog. It was living in such close proximity to Lennon that had her all

tangled up… and a little too warm… for her peace of
mind.

Chapter Five

A glance through the kitchen door showed no sign of Edie, and Lennon pulled out his phone. As soon as Sully answered, Lennon got straight to the point.

"I need the all surveillance cameras on the following two streets wiped." He named them.

"What the hell did you do?" Sully asked at once.

"Just tell me you'll handle it."

"Jesus. Are you undercover or something too now?"

He threw a look toward the kitchen, but the coast was still clear, Edie was in her room probably putting the bed together. "Look, something came up and I had to get a person out. I'm not sure of any details yet—I'm still working on that. But I don't want any footage of those streets to be searched."

"You don't want anybody knowing who got her out," Sully said.

"Who said it was a her?"

"Dude, it's always a woman." Amusement tinged his leader's tone. "All right, I'll call in on a favor one of the techies owes me. Consider it done."

"Good. And something else, Sully."

"What is it?"

Lennon picked up the tongs and flipped the steaks. "I'd like to hire a bodyguard. Who do you know?"

"Penn," he said without hesitation.

Lennon issued a quick breath. "I never thought of your brother, but yeah. I'd trust him with my life." Penn Sullivan had joined them on one of the Ranger Ops' very first missions, and he'd fit right into the brotherhood. He couldn't ask for better than the man who did this sort of thing for a living.

"I'll send him your way, all right? But in return, you tell me what the fuck's going on." Sully's tone brooked no argument.

"I don't have anything to hide from you, man. Don't get your panties in a twist."

"Asshole." He chuckled. "I'll take care of this. You take care of… whatever it is you've got going on. Call if you need me, Lennon."

He quickly ended the call and checked on the steaks again. His mind was far from food and on one beautiful little blonde in his guest bedroom at this very moment. She hadn't said a word about her troubles, but he'd bet his sidearm that she hadn't been evicted — she just needed to bug out of her apartment because she was now a target, just like the senator.

In order to really protect her, he'd have to drag the details from her. Putting her at his house with a

106

bodyguard behind the scenes wasn't enough if he didn't know what he was up against.

How to get her to talk, though? If only she'd let him get to know her better all the times before this. Dammit, frustrated wasn't even coming close to what he was feeling right now.

The back door creaked open, and he glanced up with a smile. She stood there, looking unsure, her teeth clamped on her lower lip and the dog at her side.

"He already claimed you," Lennon said.

She looked down at the dog and rubbed his ear. Ranger leaned into her hand.

Was it possible to melt at a woman's affection for his dog? If so, he just did it. His chest felt too tight— and his jeans as well after getting a good healthy look at her round curves in jeans and a simple top. Her hair waved at the ends, brushing her collarbones.

He wanted to skim her warm flesh with his lips, his tongue...

"Get settled?" he asked to break the silence.

She nodded. "The bedding is actually quite pretty. But I see why it isn't your thing."

"Yeah, Momma is very giving. Can I get you a drink? Some sweet tea?"

"I'd love some tea."

She followed him back into the kitchen, where he poured two tall glasses. He turned to her. When she accepted the glass, he lifted his forefinger and trapped hers against the glass.

Her gaze shot to his.

"Thank you for taking on my dog." He let her go.

She moved to lean against the counter opposite him. A few steps and he could have her in his hold, lips over hers, lifting her to the surface to peel away her clothes.

This was going to be one hell of a challenge. Having a beautiful, sexy woman in his home was hard enough, but one who knotted him up this bad would take a feat of willpower.

He would have to turn to exercise to get out his frustrations—either that or become a teenaged boy again, locked up in the bathroom for hours at a time while images of her sweet mouth played through his mind.

He covered his groan with a sip of tea.

"I'm glad Ranger likes me. I wouldn't make a very good dog sitter if he doesn't. When do you work?" she asked.

He lifted a shoulder and let it fall. "They call when they need me. There's no set time, which is my problem. I sort of need somebody at my beck and call. The last girl did great for a while, but she was finding she had very little personal life if she had to check on Ranger several times a day."

"That won't be a problem for me," she said at once.

He examined her closer. Part of his training was to note when people were nervous or afraid. He'd seen his share of hostages who'd been told to pretend all was well, and he didn't like how close Edie came to this.

He set aside his glass. "I'd better check the steaks. Would you mind getting out some place settings?"

"Sure."

"Just rummage around the cupboards till you find what you need. Then you'll know your way around the kitchen."

He walked out back again, and Ranger followed. As he removed the steaks from the grill and placed them on a platter, he tried to figure out how the hell to break Edie—to get her to spill to him. Only time and trust would do it, but they didn't have time to build trust.

He only hoped shielding her and getting Penn on her six would be enough to protect her from the truth he feared.

* * * * *

Edie's nerves were kicked into high gear. She prided herself on being a confident woman who handled herself, but she had never felt so... lost.

So far, Lennon had been great. He was giving her space and not prying, though she was aware of how odd this entire situation was. She probably could have gone about laying low in a dozen different ways, but Lennon's offer had given her a quick out.

Out of her apartment.

Out of her life.

Now she was outside of town staying with a man nobody would ever link her to, except maybe Hallie.

And all Edie's reasons for denying this man's advances before now seemed stupid and trivial. Yet he'd kept coming at her with sweet or silly texts. His interest was genuine, and she'd spent weeks denying her own for him.

She shot him a look from beneath her lashes. The darkened living room sent shadows over his rugged features, and his five o'clock shadow tormented her.

Seated at the other end of the sofa, he turned his head to look at her. The colors from the TV screen played over his face, but she saw the light in his eyes.

Very slowly, as if trying not to frighten her, he got up and moved closer on the sofa. When he reached for her face, she let her eyes slip closed. What was the point in fighting her attraction? She might be dead by morning if the group targeting her father found her.

No, she couldn't continue making bad decisions and place Lennon in danger too.

She opened her eyes. "Lennon, it's not a good idea for us…"

His big hand cradled her cheek and jaw. A feeling of overwhelming tenderness washed through her.

Without a word, he scooted even closer, closing the gap between them. As he leaned in and crushed his lips over hers, she let out a gasp of desire.

It was as if they were still standing on that creek bank, tearing at each other's clothes. She wanted him just as bad as that moment without any warmup at all.

She moved into the kiss. He angled her head to deepen it, and she parted her lips. The swipe of his tongue over hers made her moan.

He grabbed her by one hip and yanked her across his lap to straddle him. His bulge was unmistakable, and her panties flooded. Need clashed like waves against a rocky cliff.

"Lennon, we…"

"Can't, I know. Shouldn't, for sure. But I don't play by the rules. I thought you didn't either." He drew back to look into her eyes.

His masculine scent and the taste of him rushed over her. She lifted her hands to his angled jaw and leaned in again.

"I don't." She did anything to get her story. Was doing anything to feel good much different? Lennon was offering her all the pleasure she could handle.

She ground down on his erection, and he groaned. His fingers worked under her hair, and she loved the tugging of the strands. It made her feel…

Alive.

She ran her hands down his broad shoulders to his hard pecs. God, what did he do for a living? Government agency, her ass. He had the body of a soldier, professional athlete or maybe a construction worker. And she was determined to feel every single inch.

Her fingertips trailed over his washboard abs, each ridge igniting her further.

He kneaded her waist and then moved upward to brush his knuckles over the sides of her breasts. A shiver ran through her.

"God, I've wanted you for weeks, baby." His growled words spiked her need even more.

"I didn't call you back, because I was afraid I'd throw myself at you," she said between kisses. It was a truth she hadn't dared to let her mind touch on before now.

He nibbled down her chin to her throat. She tipped her head back, and he cradled her head in his hands as he sucked and kissed a blazing path over her skin to her breasts.

She cried out as he closed his fingers around one nipple through her bra even as he dipped his tongue into her cleavage.

"If you want to stop, it has to be now," he grated out.

She drew her head up to look at him. "I want you, Lennon."

He made a sound in his throat and lifted her at the same time he stood. She wrapped her arms around his neck and her thighs around his strong hips. He went still for a moment, gazing into her eyes. "You're sure, Edie? This complicates things."

"Don't worry — I'll still walk your dog." She found a genuine smile spreading over her face.

He started toward his bedroom. She clung to him and buried her lips against his neck, running her tongue up to his ear. He tasted of salt and man, a heady combination.

When he nudged open his door, Ranger tried to follow, but he kicked the dog out and lay Edie on his bed.

"Poor Ranger," she said breathlessly as he hovered over her, elbows holding his weight.

"Poor Edie. I bet you're aching for me to touch you here." He cupped her breast and swiped his thumb over her crested nipple. She moaned. "And here." He moved his hand down along her ribs, up under her top. His heavy, warm touch made her suck in a sharp breath. "And here." He moved his palm downward, over her mound and between her thighs.

He looked into her eyes as he applied pressure with his palm to her pussy. Even through her jeans it was driving her insane.

She shuddered with delight and clamped her fingers onto his shoulders. "I want all of it."

"Good." He did an erotic push-up, chest brushing her breasts, thighs trapping hers and his arousal grinding into the seam of her jeans. Then he began to kiss her again, with long passes of his tongue as he slowly and methodically stripped her.

Her top went first and next her bra. Her breasts seemed made for his hands—he cradled them and teased them for long minutes before finally lowering his lips to take one nipple into his mouth.

She clutched at his spine and lost herself to sensation. Nothing mattered right now but being with Lennon. Giving herself up to him felt like the only good decision she'd made lately.

When his warm, wet tongue circled her hard nipple, she cried out. He sucked with soft pulls of his mouth, his stare holding her in place. When he grazed her straining bud with his teeth, she cried out again. "More!"

He moved to the other breast, teasing it with flicks of his tongue. Just when she thought she'd die if he didn't suck on her nipple, he clamped down on it and did just that.

She threw her head back, lost to sensation. She barely remembered her working his shirt over his head, but suddenly she was touching all that hard muscle she'd only felt under clothes before now.

"I have to look at you," she bit off.

A crooked smile captured his lips, and he pushed back off the bed to stand at the edge. She sat up and moved close to him, eyes fixed on his torso. When she brushed her fingers over the chiseled muscles, she let out a sigh.

"How did you get such a body?"

"Hard work." His eyes were lidded as he watched her explore each ripple of muscle to his waist.

She unbuttoned his jeans, and he froze, hardly even drawing breath. As she lowered his zipper, she looked up into his eyes. They were two hazel flames burning down at her, and she was already on fire for him. That look built an inferno of need inside her.

"Stop," he said tightly.

She blinked at the command.

"I'm not ready yet. I want to taste you first."

* * * * *

Lennon's grip on his control was like hanging by the fingertips on a ledge, about to plunge a thousand feet. Edie's fingers brushing over his fly nearly had him at his snapping point. Sweat beaded on his forehead.

Get a grip – now.

He held her face in one palm as he started from the top by kissing her again. Damn, he didn't want to stop. She gave back nibble for nibble, swipe for swipe, and he couldn't get close enough to her.

He lowered her to the bed again and scooted her up to the pillows. Looking down at her beautiful face on his pillow was a moment that... well, he couldn't explain why his throat was suddenly tight.

"I need you, Lennon." Her soft plea edged deeper into his mind, flicking one more of his fingertips off that ledge.

With a growl, he claimed one nipple and then the other, moving back and forth until each peak was rosy red. He went for her jeans. In seconds he had her fly open and the moment he teased his fingers under the elastic of her panties, his heart started to beat out of rhythm.

Past the bare velvety skin of her mound and traveling over her seam, slick with her juices.

"You're so fucking hot and wet," he ground out.

She arched her back and rocked into his touch.

He was a goner.

In a blink, he stripped her bare. Jeans and panties in a wad on the floor and his hands locked onto the fullest part of her hips. He looked from her eyes down her beautiful body to the gorgeous feast before him.

His breaths came faster as he caught the scent of her arousal. Gently, he parted her thighs. She did the rest by pulling her knees up, exposing the slick folds of her pussy.

"You're just begging for my tongue, baby."

"Lennon!"

He went for her inner thigh first. She cried out as he sucked on the smooth flesh there, tracing a path up to the place she wanted his mouth most. But he wasn't ready to give her what she wanted quite yet.

Her stomach dipped on a gasp of air. He kissed down her thigh and back up. She latched her hand onto the back of his head, but he wouldn't be guided. Not yet.

With the point of his tongue, he trailed a line over her mound and over to her other thigh. He repeated the torment three times, then four.

He wanted her writhing for him, crying out his name when he finally buried his tongue in her soaking pussy.

"I didn't realize you're a tormenter," she rasped.

He rumbled a chuckle against her thigh. "You're getting me, baby. This is how I play. How much can you take?"

"Not much. I've been waiting since..." her words cut off on a gasp, "that reception."

"Just what I wanted to hear." Watching her face, he thumbed apart her pussy lips and blew a warm breath over her folds. Her hard clit begged for his tongue, and he was teasing himself too with this extended foreplay—his cock throbbed, trapped inside his jeans.

She trembled under him, thighs tensed.

He lowered his mouth and kissed her pussy. The soft brushing over her clit had her bucking upward

117

and moaning. He held her tight and continued to press soft kisses down the length of her seam. At the bottom, his lips and jaw were coated with her juices, and he couldn't hold back anymore.

He dived in. Lifting her ass in his hands, he licked at her neediest spots. She clenched and released under the tip of his tongue, growing slipperier by the heartbeat.

She dug her fingers into his shoulder. "Lennon, I—"

The orgasm ripped through her fast—he'd made her wait too long for it—and her loud rasps of pleasure echoed in his ears even as her pussy contracted under his tongue.

He slipped a finger into her pussy. Her body clenched around him, and he withdrew it slowly before adding a second finger and thrusting back inside.

"Take me, Lennon!" Her face was flushed, her nipples primed. She was the most gorgeous thing he'd ever seen and even more responsive to his touch than he'd ever dreamed. She rocked her hips, and he captured her clit between his lips, sucking lightly as he finger-fucked her over and over.

The second release brought a feminine scream from her that made his cock that much harder. He didn't let up on her, demanding she throw away her reservations and give him this.

This trust to make her feel good.

To see her safe.

To tell him the truth.

He dragged her orgasm out for long seconds, gentling his touch to bring her down from her high. When he raised his head, her bright blue eyes were fixed on him, hazy with desire.

"I think you killed me." She flopped back.

He chuckled as he straightened to remove his jeans and underwear. Drawing his hard length out into his hand, he held Edie's gaze. "Your turn, baby. I want your lips around me."

* * * * *

She felt like a jittery bowl of jelly after two back-to-back orgasms. Never in her life had she been worked up enough to experience two in a row.

Looking at Lennon in all his naked glory, his cock longer than any she'd seen in person, thicker too, made her worry if she could handle a man like him. He was huge, demanding... and a little sadistic too in how he'd tormented her for so long.

She also wanted him like nothing else in her life.

He stood at the edge of the mattress, looking down at her with a softness in his gaze that had her stomach dipping.

Moving to a sitting position, she flattened her hands on his hard ass and drew him a step closer. With her seated on the bed, his cock was right at her mouth level, the head purple with need and veins snaking up and down the impressive length to guide her tongue.

Holding her gaze, he guided his cock to her lips. She ran her tongue over the crest, across sweet pre-cum pooled in the depression.

"Jesus Christ." He threw his head back.

Burning all over again, she parted her lips and took him inside. The spongy head filled her mouth and hit the back of her throat, but there was so much she couldn't fit. On a moan, she began to draw on him even as she wrapped her fingers around his base. Musky male scents hit her in a cocktail too exciting to even put words to.

She moved down his length and back up to the tip, where she swirled her tongue. She didn't get to tease him for thirty seconds before he was stepping back. She stared at his erection bobbing on those glorious six-pack abs of his.

He released a rough noise and grabbed her up. Her spine hit the mattress, and he wedged himself between her thighs. As he looked down into her eyes, he slipped on a condom he must have been holding the entire time. It was impossible to look away from the tendons of his forearm as he situated the rubber to the base of his cock.

He pulled her up and into him with one hard thrust. Filling her to places that had been untouched until now, he swiveled his hips. She clutched at his shoulders and brought his mouth back to hers.

Having a man like Lennon buried inside her, claiming her with lips, teeth, tongue and cock... she didn't know how she'd ever be able to not tell him the truth now. She felt too close to him to keep secrets.

With a moan, she swirled her tongue over his and pushed down on his cock. He groaned, the rumble of his chest exciting a gasp from her. The bed shook. Outside the door, Ranger whined.

Lennon shot Edie a grin before kissing her again. The wildness of the moment blossomed and then suddenly, she was coming again. This time, her mind blanked and she only saw hazel eyes, tasted Lennon on her lips.

He let loose, jerked hard in her arms and collapsed forward, head bowed as he pumped his own release into her. Her insides gave another hard clutch at his cock and bliss washed through her body.

Edie's heart took over, and she pulled his head down to her chest and wrapped her arms around him to hold him there.

But he wasn't moving. Clearly, they were equally matched in stupidity.

Chapter Six

Lennon heard the click of the front door shutting, and he was on his feet before his eyes even opened. Edie wasn't in the bedroom.

Striding out of the room, he threw a glance at the guest room door, but he could see the bed was untouched and Edie wasn't there.

He called out for Ranger, who came to him.

"Well, she didn't take you for a walk, did she, boy?" He rushed to throw on his jeans and shoes before running out the front door.

Edie was standing on the front lawn, talking to a young kid. Her soft voice came to Lennon, but he couldn't make out what they were talking about. Lennon closed the front door, and she and the kid who couldn't be more than fifteen looked up at him. The kid's face scorched red, and he backed up a step.

Edie turned to him and rested a hand on his arm before walking back up to Lennon's house. "Good morning, Lennon," she said as she breezed past him to rub Ranger's ears. "Good morning to you too." She twisted to glance at Lennon. "I already took him for his morning walk, but I put him inside so he could drink while I talked to Jordan."

He followed her and Ranger into the house. "Jordan. Do you know that kid?" He closed and locked his door, eyeing her up. She was wearing workout pants and a T-shirt with a saying on it about journalists doing it better knotted at her waist. A sliver of skin between her top and bottoms drew Lennon in.

"I do now," she answered. "Are you a coffee drinker? I am. I hope you have some." She took off for the kitchen.

Stunned that she'd scoffed off the entire thing with Jordan and that she hadn't told him why she was talking to the young kid, Lennon strode after her. She was opening cupboards, looking for coffee.

"I don't drink the stuff, but I have some of those... pod things you put in that." He pointed to a machine on his counter. "Also a gift from Momma."

"Well, she set you up to have a great night's sleep and a great morning." She threw him a smile that hit him square in the chest.

She set me up to give YOU a great night and a great morning.

He'd have to thank his momma later.

Reaching onto a top shelf, he pulled down a box of assorted pods for the machine. Edie took it and immediately rummaged in the box to find her flavor of choice.

"Oh, there's tea too. I'll have that later." She walked over to the coffee machine, giving Lennon a view of her round ass in those clingy workout pants.

"What were you talking to that kid about?"

"He lives a few houses down and while I was walking Ranger, I ran into him." She returned to the cupboard holding the mugs and took one out. "He asked if he could mow the lawn."

He stared at her as she chewed her lip. "You know I like mowing my own lawn. I told you yesterday."

"Yes, but he's trying to earn money, Lennon. I asked what the cause was, thinking he just needed it to buy a new skateboard or spend it on his girlfriend." She folded her arms over her chest with an expression of outrage. "Do you know what he needs the money for?"

Lennon was getting deeper into this woman by the second. The look of fiery anger in her eyes was enough to bring him a step closer to her.

She whirled to the counter again and grabbed her now full mug. "His lunch account at the school is in arrears, and his family can't afford to pay. If he doesn't pay, he can't eat lunch this upcoming school year. So he's mowing lawns to earn money to pay the bill."

"Damn. Poor kid."

"I know! I'm outraged a school would do this. Lunches should be free, provided by taxpayer money.

I have half a mind to write this story and expose the entire system to the ridicule it deserves!"

Lennon wanted to smile but held it in check. He didn't want her to think he was laughing at her statements, when it was the fire in her that was making him happy. Damn, she was beautiful when outraged, her cheeks flushed and that point of her chin tipped up in defiance.

He wished the Ranger Ops had actually been called to the rally so he could have seen her in action on that stage.

He cleared his throat. "Life's not fair, that's for sure, and it's good the kid is resourceful—it will see him through the tough times. He'll need that. I think I could forego mowing the lawn a few times to give him work."

She suddenly set down her mug and threw her arms around his neck.

Lennon brought his arms around Edie, hauling her against his chest. Her soft breasts gave him a thrill.

"Thank you, Lennon."

"This right here is enough thanks, if I needed it. But I don't. I'm glad to help Jordan's cause. The kid's really going to be crushing on you when he's cutting the grass and you're home." He grinned.

"He's fifteen."

"Clearly you don't have a brother. If you did, you'd know fifteen-year-old boys crush on pretty women no matter what their ages."

A shadow crossed Edie's face, and she dropped her gaze to stare at his chest. "No, I don't have any brothers." She pulled from his arms and returned to her coffee mug. As she sipped, he watched her closely.

Son. Of. A. Bitch.

He hadn't wanted to be right about her tie to Senator Arthur, but the look on her face made Lennon pretty fucking certain he was.

"Edie," Lennon said quietly.

She looked up.

He turned to the counter and drew his computer tablet into his hands. A few swipes had him pulling up the image of her at the rally. He swallowed hard before turning it in his hands to show her.

"When are we going to talk about this?"

* * * * *

She dropped the coffee mug, and it struck the floor with a *clunk*. Hot coffee spilled out, some hitting her shin.

Her heart was just as shattered, though. She'd believed she was safe here with Lennon, far from the troubles plaguing her. How wrong she was.

She crouched to grab the broken pieces of the mug, but Lennon squatted before her and stopped her with his hands on her shoulders.

Looking down into her eyes, he said, "Leave it," and drew her to her feet again. Taking her by one hand, he led her to the living room.

Her heart was thumping so hard, she could hardly breathe. Her mind was blank even as it sped along pathways she never believed she'd have to navigate.

He knew. He'd put it all together.

Which meant so many others had as well. Her mother and the senator... even her half-siblings who didn't know a thing about her existence, would all be affected.

I've messed up, but I can't go back and fix yesterday. Only today.

How did she go about that? She hoped Hallie came through with that informant soon.

Lennon took her into the living room and drew her down to sit on the sofa. He sat next to her, staring at her for a long minute.

Finally, he dragged his fingers through his hair, making it stand on end. "Look, Edie. I think we both need to come clean with each other."

She jerked to her feet, backing away a step as panic set in. What was this? Was he part of some group—maybe even the very one targeting the senator?

"Jesus, Edie, don't look at me like that. I'd never hurt you—ever. I thought you knew that. Hell." He stood and caught her in his arms.

For a moment, she didn't know if she should succumb to the protection he offered or shove him away.

He went still, loosening his hold enough that she could pull free if she wanted. She didn't—yet. She still needed to hear what he had to tell her.

"You don't really believe I'm the bad guy, do you? Jesus, Edie. I'm here to help you."

She swallowed hard. After a few seconds, she nodded. "I'll listen to what you have to say."

This time when he sat with her, he pulled her across his lap, her legs dangling over his hard denim-clad thighs. He trailed his fingers down her spine, moving up and down until she felt herself begin to relax.

"I'll start, okay? Maybe it will make things easier for you."

"I-I don't know if I want to hear your story," she said with a tremor in her voice.

He pushed out a long sigh. "I didn't have a clue who you were when we met at Big Mike's. I was just in town visiting my mother and avoiding my real reason of being there, which was to visit Adam's grave. So I came down to have a beer and shoot the shit with some old friends."

She nodded. "And I was only there with Hallie, because she wants me to love the country like she does."

His eyes burned into hers. "I wanted to see more of you. I tried again and again, in case you hadn't noticed."

She dropped her gaze. "I did."

"Then when you wanted a date to the reception, I thought what the hell, she's beautiful and I'm single. And I needed a distraction from thoughts of my buddy who died."

She felt herself drawn to comforting him and placed a hand over the back of his. He turned his palm up and laced their fingers. Talking this way, with her curled close to him, somehow made it all seem less frightening.

"What I'm saying is, I had no idea who you are, Edie, besides somebody I wanted to know a hell of a lot better. But you see, I wasn't completely open with you about my line of work. I do work for a government agency — and that agency is Homeland Security."

She gaped at him.

"I'm in a special forces unit, a Southern division. We were formed to battle terrorism in Texas and the bordering states. But it isn't common knowledge and has to remain that way."

Good God. Of all the things he might have told her, she never could have guessed this. It took her a long minute to process his words.

Of course she wouldn't tell, and she sure as hell would never put fingers to the keyboard with this topic in mind. Lennon was trusting her by telling her, and that brought her even closer to him than last night when he'd known exactly what to do to make her feel amazing.

"The team's called Ranger Ops. See, we were all Texas Rangers before this."

"It's why you have no clue when you'll be called out," she said in quiet amazement.

He nodded. "Ranger really does need a sitter. I wasn't lying."

She saw now that he'd never lied to her, only withheld what he needed to.

"Twice, we've been called in to end things when Senator Arthur was in trouble. We rescued his nephew from those hostages a few months back."

Her eyes flew open wide.

"And we were on standby to put a stop to things at that speech Saturday."

"Oh my God. You were there and saw me get onstage." Her fingers twitched, and he tightened his grasp on them.

"No, we were on standby, not actually there in the arena. I didn't see you, but as a team, we keep abreast of all current events, and you're pretty unmistakable on the front page of every newspaper in the state."

A shudder ran through her, partly from the danger hanging over her head and partly because it was a relief that somebody in the world knew what was happening to her.

Someone who had the power — and team backing him — to *truly* keep her safe.

"Jesus, you're a hero, out saving people," she said. "Is that why you came for me?"

He caught her gaze. "You know I've been trying to win you over long before that. But yes, my only thought was to react to the alarm bells blaring in my mind. I knew this couldn't be good, you being linked to Senator Arthur and all the trouble in his house. But of course, this is all speculation. You haven't told me your side of the story yet."

He waited expectantly, and suddenly, her throat dried out, along with any words she was about to say.

At last, she dipped her gaze. "I'm the result of an affair between the senator and my mother, who's also a journalist, early in his career. She was following his path, and I guess things got out of hand. I've never met my father in person — until Saturday at the speech."

Lennon's palm was on her back again, soothing her with long, slow touches.

She continued, "It was stupid to get onstage, to want to throw myself in his face. I'd never met him before, you see... It was juvenile of me. I made a mistake. If I hadn't done that, nobody would have snapped those pictures, and nobody would have put us together."

She saw now that much of her last year or so had been spent trying to get closer to the man who'd fathered her, even when Edie hadn't recognized it. First via Jake and then she'd taken matters into her own hands.

Look how that turned out.

"I can help you."

She stared at him. "How?"

His crooked smile was sexy as hell and brought to mind all the times she'd seen it flash when he moved over her... inside her.

"The Ranger Ops' motto is guts and glory, that's how. We don't back down from a fight."

She shook her head. "When I met you at Big Mike's, I never suspected you were some kind of superhero."

"I'm not. I'm just good at what I do, and I have the best of the best on my six."

She'd never actually heard anybody use terms like that before except in movies.

"You have more to tell me." His gaze burrowed into her.

Exactly just how perceptive was this man?

132

She nodded. "After the speech, the senator caught me at my car. He told me to lay low, that I would be targeted. I thought he might be overreacting, and then somebody pushed a note under my front door."

He tensed beneath her. "Do you still have it?"

She nodded.

"I'd like to have it looked at later by my forensics team."

The fact he *could* get it examined later gave her another shock. Lennon was the real deal.

"What did it say?" he asked.

"To stay inside and watch my back, basically."

On the surface, Lennon acted as if she'd just told him it was sunny outside. His entire demeanor was calm and unfazed. But searching his eyes told Edie something much different.

He was angry.

Furious, even.

The depths of his hazel eyes darkened. "You're in the right place, baby. My team and I will dig around and see what we can uncover, because the authorities have allowed these attacks to go on too long. Which makes me question whose payroll they're on."

The journalist in her jerked to alertness. "You think the same group could be paying the cops to turn a blind eye?"

"It's happened before. One thing I've learned is trust no one."

"But you trusted me with your story," she said quietly.

Lennon stared into her eyes and eased a hand around her neck, stroking a warm path on her skin with his thumb. "I don't have a reason for telling you what I did, Edie. I've had other women and never felt the need to share that part of my life."

"Then why did you tell me?"

"Maybe for the same reason you came home with me today. There's just something between us." He eased closer.

And she tipped her face up to his. He captured her mouth in a tender caress that had her sighing with pleasure even as her insides knotted with want.

His lips brushed across hers gently before he pulled back. "I promise you'll be safe even if I'm not home. Don't be afraid to be here in the house alone or walk Ranger."

She blinked. "What did you do?"

"Just trust me." He slid his thumb across her lips, still damp from his kiss. Then with a passion that made her stomach bottom out with desire, he swooped in and claimed her mouth again.

There was nothing tender about it this time — it was all-consuming. Demanding.

Where she sat across his thighs, she felt his arousal. Her insides clenched, and she shifted on him.

Letting out a groan, he dragged her closer into the kiss, and she rolled her hips down against the bulge in his jeans. He slipped his tongue inside her mouth, and she opened on a gasp, inviting him in.

Their tongues tangled for long minutes, each stroke amping up the tension between them until she couldn't take it another moment.

"I want you," she whispered.

"I've been waiting to hear those words." His voice was gravel and ground glass, the rough edges heightening her awareness of this man and how much she wanted to give herself over to him, not only bodily but her safety as well.

She might pride herself on being a bold and strong woman, but this mess she was in was way beyond her skill set. She was in over her head, and fate had given her the perfect man to help.

Holding her gaze, he lifted her and flipped her onto the couch. She spun her arms around his neck and dragged him down on top of her. His weight made her feel too hot, too needy… and entirely safe.

He rocked his hips, grinding against her as he had on the dance floor what felt like months ago. How quickly her life had taken a dark turn. A few weeks ago, her only worry was uncovering stories or getting that full-time position at *Notable News*.

Lennon edged his fingers under her top, walking up her ribs to her breast. The minute his fingers closed around her nipple, she cried out. Arching, she kissed him with all the need building inside her and gripped his bare shoulders.

Five more shoves of his erection against the V of her legs was too much—she went for his jeans. A couple flicks of her fingers and his hard cock was spilling into her hands. She couldn't wrap her fingers all the way around his girth, but he still liked her touch, if his moan was anything to go by.

She stared into his eyes and gave him a stroke from base to tip. His eyes fluttered, and he rolled off. With quick jerks, he removed all her clothes. Then he tugged her to the edge of the sofa, spread her legs and sank his tongue into her wet, needy, aching folds.

* * * * *

Edie's sweet flavors coating his tongue had Lennon throbbing faster than a bullet expelled from a weapon. He parted her petal-soft outer lips and lapped a path around her opening, up through her wet folds to her hard clit.

Fuck, she was so slick and ready. He wanted to bury himself balls-deep—now. But he'd be lying if he said he didn't want to spend half his days feasting on her pussy and the other half inside her. To hell with sleep, food or Ranger Ops.

She tipped her hips upward, and he drew on her clit with gentle, teasing pulls of his lips. Her thighs quivered around his ears, and his own cock bobbed against his abs.

Opening his mouth wide, he flattened his tongue against the seam of her pussy, his upper lip still covering her hard pearl. She swirled her hips, and he pulled back to gaze at her.

Her eyes burned with intensity, and her pale hair tumbled around her flushed face. Her nipples jutted up toward the ceiling, dark pink. And her stomach dipped sharply with each labored breath she took.

Her pussy begged for his mouth. And his fingers.

He trailed two through her juices, zigzagging down her pussy to her opening. As he thrust them high against her inner wall, he watched her expression shatter into one of bliss. Her eyes rolled back, and she bucked into his hand.

The wet sound of his fingers inside her brought a growl to his lips. He needed to feel her clenching, and while she still pulsated with her orgasm, he was going to sink his cock into her.

He withdrew his fingers and stuck them in his mouth. She opened her eyes to catch him licking each digit clean down to the knuckle.

"Oh my God," she burst out.

"You taste too damn good." Holding her stare, he found his jeans. He pulled his wallet from his back pocket and located a condom. When he tore open the packet, his hands shook, but he managed to pull out the condom and fit it over the head of his cock. As he jerked it down over his length, he plunged his fingers inside Edie again.

Her head fell back, and she opened to him. With each withdraw of his fingers, she arched up to follow him. He added his thumb over her clit and ground it into her body.

The first shocks of her impending release hit his fingers. She trembled in his hold.

And he went wild with the need to get inside her while she was still pulsating.

He finger-fucked her deeper with every pass, his thumb circling her clit. When she gave a muffled noise, he felt the tight squeezes of her inner walls around his fingers. Two, three…

Quickly, he pulled free and drove his cock into her.

Her eyes popped open with surprise, and she surged upward, arms around his neck, mouth on his as her orgasm shook her in his arms. Biting back his need to blow, he closed his eyes on the sensation of her coming apart around him.

He began to move, hips churning, ass muscles tensing and releasing as he fucked her. She was soaking, and he didn't realize what was happening until she called out his name.

She was coming again.

Jesus, he wasn't going to last.

He roared as spurts of cum jetted from his cock, never slowing, wanting more, deeper, faster.

All of her.

She sagged in his hold, and he drew her mouth to his. The thrum of pleasure in his veins mingled with an intense need to protect this woman, a combination he'd never known before.

It was more powerful than he expected. It made his chest tight with emotions he couldn't label.

In the pocket of his jeans feet away, his phone buzzed.

Edie looked at him.

"I have to take this." He carefully separated their bodies and reached for his phone.

Penn's there.

Sully's text brought him back to the present situation. The danger coming at Edie was real. But at least they had Penn as backup.

Thanks, man. I owe you.

Don't worry – I'll collect when I'm ready.

Lennon grunted with amusement and tucked his phone away again. Then he stood, eyeing the beautiful woman still sprawled out on his sofa. "How does a shower sound, and then we'll take Ranger for a walk? I'll show you our route."

Her blue eyes cleared of the worry he'd seen there when he'd gotten the text. "Yes, that will be nice."

As soon as he pulled her to her feet, he took one look at her body and was aching all over again.

Having her wet and soapy wasn't going to help that, but he wasn't about to miss his chance.

* * * * *

Ranger jumped around her and Lennon, his leash dangling from his jaws.

Edie chuckled. "I think he's excited."

"He's always up for a walk, aren't ya, boy?" Lennon rubbed his ears and took the leash from him. Ranger held completely still as he hooked the end to his collar.

"He's well-trained."

"Surprising how quick he learned, since he was stuck in a kennel for the first nine months of his life. I got him from a rescue, and he'd been treated for malnutrition and sores from the bars of the cage."

Her stomach hollowed out. "I hate stories like that. They're all too common. He's lucky to have you."

"I'm lucky to have him."

They walked outside and when Lennon entered an alarm code, he made sure she saw it. He looked to her.

"Did you remember that?"

"Yes." She tapped her temple to indicate the digits were stored away.

"Arm it every single time you go out."

"I will."

When they reached the sidewalk, he turned his head to glance over his shoulder and then continued on, Edie next to him and Ranger out in front leading

140

the way. The neighborhood was quiet. Birds chirped, and the sound of traffic seemed muffled.

"This is a nice area to raise a family."

He stared at her.

God, had she blurted that out? Now he probably thought she was digging for more from him, when that wasn't the case at all. She only planned to stay here for a few days, until the senator and whatever authorities were on the case settled things. Then she'd return to her life.

"It is a nice place. I chose it for security reasons. I've seen too much working as a state trooper and then Texas Ranger."

Their pace was leisurely, and the dog settled in. Lennon turned the corner, and they made their way down another residential street. On the opposite side of the street, an older lady was out walking her dog too, a toy poodle the size of Ranger's head. Lennon lifted a hand to her in greeting.

"You get to know these people, though we never speak." He slanted a smile at Edie.

"Lennon." Her heart pounded with fear at the thought in her head. "What if someone follows me?"

"They won't."

"But how can you be so sure?"

He glanced over his shoulder again. She followed his gaze but saw nothing. "Trust me, okay? I won't let anything happen to you. I promise."

She didn't know where he got his assurance on the topic, but she had no choice than to believe him.

"When do you think you'll leave the house again?" she asked.

Ranger took a left, knowing this route blindfolded.

"I'm never sure. It could be in ten seconds or ten days. Usually, a week doesn't pass with me at home, though."

"How long do you go for?"

He shrugged. "As long as it takes."

Her mind was all over this story. As a journalist, she liked to dig into the lives of people who fought for and protected their country. She was definitely curious about things Lennon had done. But of course she wouldn't ask him.

Knowing she'd slept with a man who had this much control and power too... damn, it was hot. She wasn't a girl whose head was easily turned, and she always went for the smarts in men, though it was clear Lennon wasn't only a muscled man who was good with weapons. It took a very high intellect to perform his job.

"Ranger never seems to slow," she noted to make conversation.

Lennon laughed. "I'd like to see the person who can wear this dog out. I've tried."

"I can't believe that. You have a lot of stamina." A flush scorched her face as she realized what she'd said and how it sounded. She stole an apologetic look at him.

He arched a brow, the corner of his mouth quirked. "I'll take that as a compliment."

They walked on and eventually her face cooled.

"Hallie told me a little about you in high school."

He grunted. "I hate to hear what was said."

"Only that every girl chased after you and your brother."

He gave a noncommittal shrug.

"Does he live around here?"

"Few minutes away. Edie, what do you know about the senator's children?"

His question slapped her, and she missed a step of their pace. He paused until she was beside him again.

"I only know what I've read."

"Never met them?"

She shook her head.

He continued walking in silence, making the last corner to lead them home.

"Why?" she asked after a minute.

"Just wondered."

She didn't think he was only questioning her to satisfy his curiosity, though. Lennon wasn't a man who wasted words. His question had her thinking hard about all she knew about the senator's son and daughter as they walked back to the house and even later on as she got Ranger a drink of water and she sipped some from a glass with ice.

Lennon disappeared for a spell, and she had to wonder what he was up to.

If she asked, would he tell her? She had a feeling Lennon wasn't always an open book, and the secrets he kept would be buried too deep for her to dig out.

Chapter Seven

Lennon leaned his elbows on the tabletop, his gaze moving from one man on his team to the next. Each one was paying attention to every word he said.

"We've got to dig deep and find out everything we can." He tapped the table with a palm to punctuate his point. "A threat's brewing just under the surface. All it takes is that rebel group to cook one bomb and then hundreds of Senator Arthur's supporters are dead. We can't wait for that to happen. This isn't only about Edie."

Sully leaned back in his chair with a nod. "You're right. I'll contact a few people about going deeper to see what we can find."

Lennon turned to Jess. "Hack whatever mainframes you need to—just get that information."

Jess shot him a grin but hid it the moment Lennon caught him.

"What's that for?" Lennon asked.

"Didn't think I'd see the day you were playing house with a woman."

"We're not playing house—I'm keeping her safe while we sort through this shit."

"Are hickeys part of the safety part then? I sure hope you're being 'safe', man." Jess reached out and pressed a forefinger into the side of Lennon's neck.

He slapped him away, but he felt the heat rising in his face. Across the table from him, Linc was giving him a shit-eating grin.

"I'm not joking about any of this, guys. We need a team on the case and when we get what we need, we move in and end it. This shit's gone on far too long. The senator has been living in fear for a year at least."

"Lennon's right," Sully said. "Linc, you and Shaw dig up everything you can on the weapons used in the attacks against the senator. Jess, Cav, you work your magic with the computers. Hack into the senator's fucking phone if you have to. We're looking for any unusual ties to people who might be selling weapons, importing them illegally or producing them."

Jess gave a sharp salute and stood. "On it, boss man." He and Cav moved out to the room where the computers were set up for just this purpose.

"Guys," Sully said to Linc and Shaw.

The two heaved themselves to their feet and left the room.

Lennon was left with Sully to stare at him.

"Say what's on your mind, man," Lennon said at once.

Sully let out a long sigh. "We have to entertain the thought that no matter how much effort you put into this, that we won't be able to protect her."

Lennon exploded to his feet, gaze fixed on his commander. "We're the goddamn Ranger Ops—we don't fail. Why are you saying this?"

"For a while, I've suspected everything isn't on the up and up with Senator Arthur. If it was, why isn't the government doing more to protect him and his family?"

"The family is *innocent*, Sully. Just like your family."

"Yeah, but there's something more to Arthur. He's dirty."

"If he is, then he'll get what's coming to him. But Edie shouldn't be looped into that category."

"She's a journalist. How do you know she isn't just out to get a story from this, Lennon?"

"Jesus. I thought you were the most levelheaded among us, Sully. Listen to yourself. Nobody wants to put herself into the crosshairs just to get a story."

Slowly, Sully got to his feet. Their gazes clashed. "Man, I've got your back. I got you Penn, didn't I?"

Lennon said nothing.

"Look, I'm just thinking of every angle. It's my job."

Lennon clenched his jaw against any angry comment he might make. He knew Sully was just covering their bases—he was Ranger Ops. They overturned every stone and did enough legwork on their missions to circle the globe before ever making a move.

But he wasn't going to make Edie out to be some journalist rabid for a story and putting herself into the danger just to experience it firsthand or to write about Ranger Ops.

"She admitted she made a bad decision, that it might have been rash. But she only did it because the man is her father, and she's never looked him in the eyes." Lennon focused on his leader, who glanced down.

"All right. I trust you, Lennon. You know that. If you think this is what we need to do, then we'll back you up."

"'Preciate it," he said. "I'm going home and relieve Penn for a bit. The man's been there for hours."

"He's used to it. Besides, it's probably a picnic after what he just did in Colombia. I'll be in touch. Let me know if you get more intel from your woman."

Lennon stopped and turned to Sully. He opened his mouth to say she wasn't his woman, but he couldn't say the words. With a shake of his head, he left, his mind cluttered with moments with Edie where she very much felt like *his woman*.

* * * * *

"Oh my God!" Edie stared at the bits of foil from the candy bar she'd had stashed in her bag from weeks ago, long before she'd added her clothing to it and left with Lennon.

She rushed into the other room to see Ranger lying on his side, eyes closed.

"Oh no. No, no, no! Dogs aren't supposed to eat chocolate!"

But he had. The evidence was all over the floor next to her bag, and the dog was... Well, she needed to take action and fast.

She dropped to her knees next to the animal and rubbed his head. "Are you okay, buddy? Shit, you're not." She fumbled for her phone. She should call Lennon, but what if he was really out saving the world and she interrupted to tell him she'd poisoned his dog?

If she could get Ranger up, maybe she could get him into a cab. First, she had to call a cab.

She latched onto his collar and shook him a little. He didn't budge, but his breathing was fast. "Come on, Ranger. I'm so sorry, but I'll help you. Get up." When it was apparent the dog wasn't moving, she ran for her phone.

She called the first vet she pulled up in her local directory and asked what to do if a dog ate chocolate. Their answer was exactly what she knew it would be — get the dog emergency treatment right away. Things to look for were seizures, lack of responsiveness and muscle rigidity, along with vomiting and diarrhea.

Shaking, she had to figure out how to get the animal up.

Her mind latched onto the neighbor boy. If Jordan could help her lift Ranger into a cab, she could get him to the vet.

She jabbed the number for the cab service and then ran outside, ignoring Lennon's rule to arm the security system. She'd be back in seconds with Jordan.

Sprinting across the street, she pounded on the door. A woman came to answer it.

"Is Jordan home? I could use his help."

She arched a brow.

"I know he mows lawns, and I could use some help lifting something heavy into the car. Is he home?" She tossed a look over her shoulder, as if Ranger would get up and wander out on his own.

The woman hesitated before saying, "I'll get Jordan."

Relief had Edie's hands tingling, and she jiggled a foot as she waited for Jordan to appear. "I need your help!" she cried as soon as he stepped onto the porch.

She ran back to Lennon's house. Ranger hadn't moved. Jordan stared down at the dog. "What happened to him?" he asked.

"He got a chocolate bar out of my bag. I feel so terrible!" She fell to her knees next to Ranger and stroked his side. "I have a cab on the way. Can you help me lift him out and into the cab?"

"Yes."

Only a few minutes later, the cab rolled up. Jordan didn't need her help, though—he was a big, strapping boy who was able to lift the dog on his own.

After Ranger was on the back seat, Edie threw her arms around Jordan, saying she'd get him some money for compensation, and then got into the cab with Ranger.

The entire way to the vet's office, she talked to the dog. Several times, she thought of calling Lennon. But she didn't want to distract him either.

What a terrible dog sitter she was. Her first day alone with Ranger and she'd poisoned him.

Her life was really starting to be a series of bad choices. What was happening? She wasn't careless or stupid—she had to put on the brakes fast.

When reaching the vet's office, she had someone come to help her lift Ranger out of the cab. As she explained what had happened, tears started to clog her words. If Lennon lost his dog to her mistake, she'd never forgive herself. And she wouldn't expect him to forgive her either.

Their relationship would be over.

Was it a relationship? They'd had a few dates, he'd taken her in when he didn't know where else to turn, and they'd slept together. That couldn't be construed as a relationship.

But the idea of losing him bothered her—a lot.

She had to at least text Lennon and tell him something was wrong with his pet. As she removed her phone from her pocket, her hands trembled. She steadied them and found their message chain. In as few words as possible, she let him know what happened.

He responded immediately. *Which vet?*

She replied.

I'm coming.

Those two little words worried the hell out of her. As a word maven, she realized so much meaning could be behind them.

He was fraught with worry. Or angry.

She wouldn't blame him for the latter.

The veterinary team took Ranger into the back to hydrate him with IV fluids, and Edie was dumped back out into the waiting room with stacks of dog and cat magazines to hold her interest. Pets came and went with their owners, but she stared into space and prayed Ranger was all right.

A pair of legs clad in black cargo pants appeared next to her, and she jerked her gaze up the long length of Lennon. He wore a military green T-shirt stretched across his broad chest. Above that, his hazel eyes burned down into hers. He reached up to rake

152

his fingers through his hair, showing her how it had become so mussed.

She jolted to her feet. "I'm so sorry, Lennon."

His face blanked and then pain creased it. "He's..."

"No!" Oh God, he thought she was giving condolences. She grabbed both his hands. "Ranger's in getting IV fluids. They think they can flush the toxins out. I'm just so sorry that he got into my bag. I never thought about that chocolate bar being left in—"

Lennon wrapped his arms around her, crushing her against his big body. Her breath whooshed out, and she pressed her cheek to his soft shirt, allowing him to comfort her as much as he was comforting himself by holding her.

When he loosened his embrace, she looked up to find an older lady smiling at them. From the outside, she and Lennon were a loving couple worrying over their pet.

"I'm going to talk to them about Ranger." He brushed her hair off her cheek. "I'm not upset with you, baby."

She sat back down on the bench with a thud, weak after her adrenaline rush of discovering Ranger and what he'd done, getting Jordan to help and finally the hurdle of facing Lennon.

He stood at the receptionist's window, giving Edie a damn good look at his rugged beauty from behind. Under different circumstances, she might stride up to him, grab him by the hand and drag him outside to have her way with him.

Her thoughts shocked her.

A few minutes later, Lennon walked back over to where Edie sat. She scooted down the bench to make room for him, and he sank beside her. "They'll let us see Ranger in a bit when he's more stable. It seems like you found him in time and got him the help he needed." Lennon placed a hand over hers.

She pressed her lips together and battled emotion. "I let you down and—"

"No, it was a mistake. It isn't like you fed him the chocolate. He's just a scavenger. He could have eaten anything in your bag—a sock, some lipstick."

"If you want me to go and you find another dog sitter, I totally—"

He cut her off again. "No. You're great, and we're going to be okay, Edie."

She stared at his hand over hers, rolling his words around in her mind. Who was the 'we' that he referred to? He and Ranger? The way Lennon said it... she felt like she was included. Like all three of them were in it together.

* * * * *

Of all the times to get called out, Lennon could think of a few better ones.

He brought his night vision scope up and peered through it. One look at the lay of the land had him flashing back to when Linc was taken prisoner. It looked so fucking much like it that Lennon's palms started sweating.

Recalling how he'd gone fucking crazy searching for his twin and finally realized the worst had happened.

As if feeling the same, Linc clamped a hand onto Lennon's shoulder. Lennon raised a finger and twitched it to the left, where he believed the threat would come from. The right was more difficult with thick brush to navigate. And the cargo being brought through from truck to the farmhouse wasn't going to walk it easily.

Around midnight, they'd gotten the call that a group of women had been nabbed outside of Galveston, believed to be trafficked into slavery in other parts of Texas. For a while, the Ranger Ops team had been given conflicting intel on where the truck would stop, but in the end, Jess and Lennon had put their heads together and pointed at a map, and they'd been right.

It was clear this particular location had been used more than once—there were depressions of footsteps in the mud that had been made by several people, and they were all small shoe sizes.

"We've got engine noise." The declaration filled Lennon's comms unit, and he shot Linc a look. *Get ready.*

Linc gave a nod as if understanding his telepathy. The engine rumble came from far off, down one of the farm to market roads that reminded Lennon so much of home. Which led him to thoughts of Edie and the wedding reception, of wanting her so bad but trying to hold back and failing.

Now she was at home sound asleep and would wake to find the note he'd left for her and the prospect of getting Ranger home from the animal hospital by herself come morning. The dog had made a full recovery and would be released soon, Lennon had been informed the previous evening.

When he'd told Edie the good news, she'd dropped her gaze to her hands, guilt written all over her face. Lennon had a feeling that guilt was more than the mishap with Ranger—she felt like a burden to Lennon, and the only way to put a stop to that was to clear up the mess with the senator. Once Arthur was no longer in danger, Edie wouldn't be, and that meant Lennon could show her how things could really be between them.

He'd wanted her from the first time he laid eyes on her—he wasn't going to let her walk away without exploring what they could be without a dark storm cloud hanging over their heads.

His mind was shut off and only tactical maneuvers flooded in as the truck arrived on scene. He and Linc crouched and ran into position, as the rest of the team circled the truck with Shaw in a higher position with his sniper rifle in case the assholes put up a fight.

And they would — they always did.

The truck doors opened, and Lennon felt Linc stiffen at his side. Months ago, his twin had been tossed into the back of a manure truck and taken someplace where he endured torture. Linc had to be thinking about it as he looked at a similar vehicle, but he held completely still, his breathing not even audible.

Lennon gave his brother a nod. *I got your back.*

I know.

Lennon had very few people in this world to call family — Linc, his momma and his team. But after adopting Ranger, he'd come to understand why people called their pets family.

Then Edie had come into his life, dancing on the fringes of it until recently. But she was still holding herself far from him. Even after making love to her, he sensed her restraint. He couldn't help but feel there were other secrets she was keeping or even that daddy issues might be at play — feelings of unworthiness that made getting close to her impossible.

All this trickled through Lennon's mind a split second before Sully gave the signal. Lennon and his team were on their feet, weapons aimed at the driver and passenger of the truck. They shouted for the guys to freeze and drop their weapons, but one fired a shot.

Through his scope, Lennon saw the shooter.

It was a woman.

"What the fuck is going on?" Linc shouted from next to him.

"I see it too. Selling your own gender. Jesus."

A shot rang out, and he realized Shaw had taken it.

There was no time for more thoughts about his personal life. Lennon and Linc moved in. While the team subdued the drivers, Linc reached for the back door of the truck.

"Cover me."

"I got you," Lennon responded, weapon raised.

Linc flipped the lock holding the sliding door down and then shoved it upward fast. Linc shined his light inside, and the frightened faces of seven women stared back.

"On your feet if you're able and hands in the air," Lennon commanded.

"Jesus, man, look at them. They're already scared out of their minds." Linc lowered his weapon.

"One could be posing and holding a weapon. On your feet and hands in the air!" he called out.

One by one, they each got to their feet and placed their hands up. Linc jumped into the truck and frisked them all before handing them out to Lennon to assist to the ground.

While Shaw and Cav handled the dead driver, Jess and Sully moved the female sidekick up against the wall of the farmhouse and began interrogating her. Lennon and Linc got out heat wrap blankets for the women and distributed bottles of water to them.

Lennon looked down at one of the blondes huddled on the ground, his mind on another blonde. She met his gaze.

Lennon crouched before her. "What's your name?" he asked softly.

"Rachel."

"We're going to take care of you, Rachel, and make sure you get home safely."

She nodded and huddled into the foil blanket.

The rest of the night dragged on while the Ranger Ops waited for other authorities to come retrieve the dead man, the woman in custody and take care of the seven kidnapped women.

Seeing their state of terror, Lennon had never felt such a drive to protect Edie. The rebel group after the senator was capable of anything, and no way would Lennon let something like this happen to her.

* * * * *

As soon as Edie helped Ranger out of the cab, Jordan jogged across the street to greet them. He smiled at the dog, who thumped his tail.

"I'm glad to see he's okay," Jordan said.

"Me too. Such a relief." She smiled at the young man and then glanced at the grass. "Looks as if the grass could use cutting. Will you be able to get to it soon?"

"Today," he said.

"Good. Just come to the door when you're done so I can pay you."

He thanked her and jogged back across the street. She smiled to herself and then tugged gently on Ranger's leash. "C'mon, boy. Let's go home."

He wagged his tail and trotted up to the door. She punched in the alarm code and led the dog inside. As soon as he entered, she detached his leash, and Ranger ran around the house, making sure his toys were all still in the corner and his water and food bowls were in the kitchen.

Satisfied, he curled up on the rug for a snooze. She stood there watching him for a minute. With Lennon gone, she couldn't keep her mind from swaying to what he could be doing... the dangers he could be facing.

It was odd for her, worrying about someone this way. Her mother was independent and traveled often, leaving Edie with a sitter as a child. And that meant Edie had learned to rely on herself, which made it difficult for her to ask Lennon for assistance.

Of course, she hadn't asked—he'd demanded she let him do what he could for her. But after only a few days of being here, she felt antsy.

A glance at the corner of the living room where the computer was set up made her itch to get back to work.

If he hadn't thrown her out for almost killing his dog, he surely wouldn't mind her using his system.

She switched on the computer, and as it booted up, she watched Ranger again. His chest rose and fell with deep, even breathing. Suddenly, she understood why mothers watched their children while they slept. She'd only been in Ranger's life a few days, but she enjoyed his presence, his happy, tongue-lolling smiles and even how he dripped on the floor after he lapped up water from his bowl.

When she left, she'd miss him.

Leaving couldn't happen until the threat against the senator eased, and since coming here, she was too far out of the loop. She only knew the things the news reported and she read on her phone. As she waited for the computer to come to life, she scanned her emails on her phone and found one from Hallie.

When can you come to the country? I have some information.

Her heart gave a hard jerk, and she hit reply. *Not for a while. What can you tell me over email or text?*

After she hit send, she heard the lawn mower start up outside the front windows. Jordan was on his way to earning some money toward his school lunch bill.

While she waited for Hallie's return email or a text, she opened a word document and began typing up the exposé about Jordan and the school system that had practically typed itself out in her mind since the moment she'd first spoken to him.

After reading it through twice, she chewed on her lip. Ranger had flipped onto his back, his paws in the air. She smiled to see he was back to his old self and then stared at the article she'd written.

It wasn't much use without a reader. She could send it to her editor at *Notable News* and let him decide what to do about printing it. The piece was exactly what the news source liked to report besides politics and world affairs. Articles that the regular Joes of America could connect to always went over well.

Sending the article would also keep her relevant — in her editor's mind.

She tapped her fingers on the light wood desk and then opened her email and signed in. A few words to her editor along with the article attachment, and the decision was made.

She hit send and looked at the rest of her emails she hadn't opened yet, taking time to weed out junk from things she could deal with later, such as a bill that was due at the beginning of the month.

All of this felt so mundane, daily life, that it was hard to believe she was sitting in Lennon's home rather than her own apartment.

The whole situation was confusing. She'd left her place with Lennon without any attacks, which the senator had made her think could happen. She'd gone to the vet and back with Ranger without anybody following her or slipping her notes of warning.

She wasn't naïve—Lennon must have something to do with it. How wide was his reach, anyway?

Her phone gave her a notification of a new email. Quickly, she signed out of her account online and opened it on her phone.

What part of the city are you in?

Edie responded rapid-fire, her heart beating fast.

The note from Hallie took only a minute to arrive in Edie's mailbox and was all of five words: Informant. Library. Ask for G.

Edie's heart pounded as she scanned those words over and over. Then she threw another look at Ranger. He was still asleep, and the vet had assured her the dog was back to normal now and could go on with his usual routine.

If she left the house for a little while, Ranger would be fine.

Decision made, she grabbed her purse and some of the cash Lennon had left for her to pay Jordan. Outside, she armed the system and ran down Jordan in the yard to pay him early. Then she set off on a brisk walk to the bus stop several streets away to go to the library and ask for G.

Chapter Eight

Lennon cussed as he called Edie for the second time in a row, and she still didn't pick up. He was also stuck in a line of traffic that would take him twenty minutes to move a fraction of a foot in, and his patience had left itself a mile back.

Where was she?

He was about to dial her a third time, when his phone buzzed in his hand. The number on it was unfamiliar, but he brought the phone to his ear.

"Reed," he bit out his last name in greeting.

"Dude, your woman's getting herself in some deep shit, and I'm about to go in there and yank her ass out."

"Penn, what the fuck's happening?" He gripped the wheel of his truck tighter, staring at the mile of traffic in front of him.

"Edie left about an hour ago."

"Left the house?" His stomach clenched at the thought of her leaving him.

"Yeah, she took off on foot and it wasn't a dog walk either. Ranger's still inside, and that kid's mowing the lawn, or was when I left to follow Edie."

"Where the hell'd she go?" His fingers ached as he tightened his hold on the wheel.

"She walked the six blocks to the bus stop. She got on and I ran to the next stop and boarded there so she wouldn't see me. She got off at the city library, went inside and asked for somebody named G."

"What. The. Fuck." Lennon clamped his jaw after each word.

"From what I'm hearing, G is some sort of informant, into some dark shit, and your little girl's stuck her boots right in it. I'm going to haul her out and spank her ass if you don't get over here right now."

Lennon glared at the taillights in front of him. "I'm going to spank her myself. Son of a bitch. I'm stuck in traffic and not getting out anytime soon. Just do your job and keep her safe. I'll handle her when I get there."

Jesus. The woman knew she was in danger — she'd knowingly gone out to look it dead in the eyes.

Lennon had never grabbed some rope and tied down a woman before, but it was sounding better and better. The longer he sat in the traffic jam, the more he wondered what the hell to do about Edie. She was clearly set on seeking answers for herself.

Could he blame her, though? Days had passed, and he was no closer to getting her safe than he was the first day he'd brought her into his home. With Ranger being in the animal clinic and then this overnight mission, he hadn't exactly been concentrating on getting to the root of her problem.

That was about to change.

He made some calls. The intel he required was within reach—his team just needed to get on it. He was on the phone with Jess the longest, and the guy was already connected to several computer systems, had hacked passwords and was downloading information as they spoke.

As soon as Lennon could get his bumper over the yellow road lines, he whipped his truck into traffic headed the opposite direction. Horns blared, and people gave him the finger as they avoided hitting him, but he didn't care—he had to reach Edie.

He folded his fingers into his palm. He could already feel her soft, plump ass under his hand.

* * * * *

Edie was utilizing every interview trick she had up her sleeve to get deeper into this woman, 'G's', head.

It seemed the woman was an ex-housekeeper of an influential man, and she'd seen things. Then she'd left the household, moved away and gone to work at the library. She had told somebody that she would be willing to talk if the time was right.

Hallie's friend of a friend had gotten the information, and here Edie sat in front of the woman, who was feigning to read a thick volume on American history.

Everything about the moment made Edie feel as if she'd fallen into somebody else's life, that she was dealing with spies and things she didn't know how to control. They were out of G's control too, by Edie's guess. If this man of power decided to come after G, he knew where she was and how to do it.

Edie flipped a page of her own book and glanced up at the woman. She was middle-aged with white threads woven through her dark hair. She didn't glance up at Edie, not once.

Barely moving her lips as she spoke, the woman managed to get out a tale about how her boss had operated an underground group. Men came at all hours to exchange money, they would go into a building on his property and then leave in trucks. She didn't know what was exchanged, but she suspected it was weapons. A few times she overheard conversations while cleaning floors and nobody thought her listening, because she wore headphones.

"Can you tell me if this man had any tie to the senator? Senator Arthur?" Edie breathed out the question.

The woman's fingers tensed on the page she was about to flip, and she gave a barely perceptible nod.

"He did not like the senator, what he stands for. He and his son spoke of it many times within my hearing."

167

Edie couldn't think of anything else she wanted to ask. She had most of what she needed — a motive for the powerful man to go after the senator and his family. An illegal weapons trade would be enough.

Edie only needed one more thing, and it was a name.

When she put the question to G, the woman went dead still for a long moment.

She held her breath.

The woman's eyelids fluttered, and she darted looks around her. When she looked into Edie's eyes, she mouthed the name.

Breckham.

The name of the man Edie herself had uncovered.

She pushed out a breath, fear turning her blood icy, and offered G a tight smile. "Thank you for this. You're very brave to speak to me."

The woman returned to her book, flipping a page, her eyes moving down the paragraphs. She did not speak again, and Edie got up, gathered her things and walked out of the library, watching her surroundings as she did.

Outside, she stopped dead in her tracks on the flight of steps leading from the library.

God, he'd found her.

Lennon's face was chiseled stone as he glared at her from dark hazel eyes. He grabbed her by the elbow, his fingers not bruising, but she knew she couldn't get away either.

"What were you thinking?" he growled, low.

"I can't talk to you about it here."

"Jesus, Edie." He hauled her down the steps and across the street. She was stuffed into his truck, and they drove in silence.

"Ranger was fine when I left him," she said at last.

He threw her a look. "This has nothing to do with Ranger, and you know it! I'm pissed off because you took a risk—a big fucking risk—in going out and meeting that informant."

Her jaw dropped. "How the hell—"

"Did you think I would leave you without protection, Edie? What kind of boyfriend would I be if I did that?"

"B-boyfriend?" she sputtered. "You're my boyfriend now? I thought I was just your dog sitter."

"You're lying to yourself if you believe we aren't more to each other. Goddammit, woman, you could have been taken off the streets. I never would have seen you again!"

She swallowed hard as she considered his words. "No matter the dangers, journalists get in there and get their story."

"This isn't about a story. Though I also know you sent one out to your editor at *Notable News* this morning."

She sucked inward on a loud gasp. "Am I a prisoner in your home? I thought I was allowed free

169

rein, *mi casa es su casa* and all that? But you're having me followed—"

"Guarded," he interrupted.

She barreled on, anger spilling over at the violation of her own first amendment rights. "And you know all my internet activity. Who the hell are you?"

He slanted a hot look at her. "You know who I am and what I have access to. My job was to protect a woman who was being targeted because of her ties to the senator, and I took that job seriously. But you're on some..." he searched for the word "...crusade to find the information all by yourself, to get it to the right people and save the senator. Maybe then he'll remember he has a daughter and want to lay claim to you!"

She cried out as the cruel remark hit home. She turned her face away and bit back her tears.

"Fuck. Edie, I'm sorry. I didn't mean that."

"Yes, you did," she said thickly. "And... I think you may be right."

He went silent, and she didn't have any words to say as they drove the rest of the way to his home. When he got out of the truck, he moved to her door and opened it. She saw him give a chin lift of acknowledgement to somebody on the street and turned to look.

The man was as tall and broad as Lennon was.

"That's the bodyguard, isn't it? You let me see him on purpose," she said.

He held out a hand to her. "Yes. C'mon."

He took her inside, and Ranger did his circles of greeting. Life was gliding along on in its usual path here in Lennon's world, and inside, she was crumbling apart.

Everything she knew about herself was in question. Lennon had brought it to light. She did want to help the senator—her father—because she hoped in some small way, he might see her as an asset to his life and want a relationship with her.

The realization made her feel weak and silly and childish.

Lennon got the dog out into the back yard to romp for a while, and then he sank to the sofa. He waved her over.

She folded her arms and stared at him. "I can talk from here."

Suddenly, he grabbed her and threw her over his lap, face down. When he rubbed his hand over her backside in a soft caress, she jerked in surprise.

"I should spank your ass for what you just pulled, but I'd rather fuck it."

She twisted in his hold, facing him and trying to scramble away, but he caught her palm and moved it to his face. Just the feel of his chiseled jaw under her hand sent a tingle through her body to match the one on her backside.

171

The heat clawing at her insides and between her thighs was unmistakable arousal.

He made a sound in his throat that made her look at him closely. "When are you gonna start trusting me?"

She opened her mouth, but no words emitted.

"Have I ever given you reason not to trust me, Edie?"

She hated how broken he sounded over it. Remorse flooded her.

"If you had just called me before going down to the library, I would have found a way to come with you."

"I didn't know where you were or what you were doing. I couldn't just pull you from a mission or whatever it is you do."

He looked into her eyes. "I'm falling in love with you, woman. I'd flip heaven and hell to help you."

His words hit her one by one, as if slow raindrops plopped over her before she could realize it was raining and move to find shelter. But she couldn't shield herself from those words—they hurt her and elated her all at the same time.

She shook her head. "You can't love me."

He arched a brow in challenge. "No?"

"No. You're just feeling these things because I'm under your roof and you've been protecting me. Or trying to."

His throat worked. "I was feeling things long before that. You coming here was just fate's way of saying we should be together, even if you're too damn driven — or stubborn — to see it."

Her heart wobbled, about to crack. Searching Lennon's eyes, she knew he'd be able to catch it before it shattered, tuck it close and keep it safe.

She just had to trust him, as he'd said.

"God, Edie. If anything had happened to you…"

"How could it have? Your bodyguard was following me."

He narrowed his eyes. "That's it — I changed my mind about spanking that round ass of yours." He threw her face-down over his lap again. This time, there was no tender caress that sent need shooting to her pussy. He brought his hand down with a slap that had her rearing back.

He brought his hand down again, but this time slipped his fingers between her thighs, rubbing her needy slit through her cotton pants. His fingertips traced the outer lines of her lips and pressed the cloth between them.

She went limp in his hold, and he made his move, turning her and settling her spine on the sofa. His dark eyes loomed close.

"Tell me you don't feel something for me, and I'll leave you alone," he said roughly.

She panted with desire and had to take precious seconds to think around the throb of need in her clit before she could find words.

He pushed away and started to leave the living room.

"Wait! Lennon." She closed her fingers around his forearm. "I'm not very good with feelings. My mother loved me, but we didn't tell each other daily, monthly or even yearly. It's just something each of us knew without saying."

"So journalists, people who know words more than others, are stingy with them. Got it."

She tightened her hold on his arm, standing to face him. "How about these words, Lennon — take me to bed."

* * * * *

Getting Edie naked took seconds but felt like hours. Each bit of flesh he revealed, he had to kiss. Some of them he licked. And when he exposed her nipples, he used his teeth.

Her gasps of delight drove him on. Dammit, he was going to make her lose her mind for him if he had to keep her in his bed day and night.

The soft brush of her fingers over his jaw jacked his need up tenfold. His cock was aching, harder than ever. And he wasn't going to wait to bury himself inside her.

He flipped her on the mattress. The golden curves of her backside had him leaking pre-cum. When she turned her head sharply on the pillow and looked at him, he looked into her eyes and fell in love the rest of the way.

"I want you, Lennon," she rasped.

He jerked the condom down over his cock with one quick flick. Then he lifted her hips and plunged inside.

Her tight, wet sheath enveloped him, and he threw his head back on a roar. Passion blasted through him along with all the restrained lust he'd battled all night without her. He cupped one of her breasts, finding the nipple and teasing it as he fucked her deeper with every pass.

The soft cries coming from her intensified. His balls swung against her pussy, and her hot juices flooded him more.

He had to look into her eyes.

As he withdrew to turn her over, her inner walls clenched around him to hold him inside. She gave a mewl of disappointment but flipped to stare up at him. What he saw in her blue eyes slammed him hard.

Reaching for him, she wrapped her arms around his neck and drew him atop her. "I'm falling for you too, Lennon."

A growl escaped his lips as he pushed her thighs apart, wedged his hips between them and thrust

175

home. Her eyelids fluttered, but she didn't look away from him as he slammed into her again and again.

She dug the points of her nails into his backside, and he ground his hips. She hooked her heels around his waist and bucked up to meet his plunges. Their lips connected in a wild dance of tongues. He felt the moment her orgasm hit.

The tightening of her pussy drove him to the finish line in a heartbeat. His cock stiffened even further, and the first jet of cum stole his breath.

She was crying out, thrashing beneath him. He continued pumping into her, slower now, drawing out both their releases.

When she went limp in his hold, he collapsed, half rolling into the bed to keep from crushing her. He opened his eyes to find her staring at him.

From the look in her eyes, he expected her to say something sweet.

"Um... the dog's looking at us."

He crumpled with laughter. She followed in a fit of giggles, and they clutched each other as they gasped and shook.

"Not a very romantic ending," he bit off between deep chuckles.

She buried her face against his chest. "No, but it's real. And we're real people. We know relationships aren't all candles and champagne bubble baths. Both of our jobs keep us down-to-earth."

He skimmed his thumb over her cheekbone, studying her eyes up close. Her irises were actually made up of several shades of blue, from turquoise to pale blue sky.

He kissed her.

She moaned and parted her lips for him to probe her tongue. The soft pulls of her lips drove him to hardness again, and soon he was reaching for another condom.

Chapter Nine

"Tell me everything you learned from your meeting." Lennon nudged open the pizza box lid and picked up two steamy slices of pepperoni and mushroom. He placed them on a dish and then handed it to Edie.

She thanked him and waited for him to get his own pizza—four slices—and they carried their plates into the living room.

She sank to the floor in front of the coffee table, and Ranger came over immediately to start begging.

"You're in trouble now," Lennon said. "He'll never leave you alone."

"I'm half afraid to feed him anything after he ate that chocolate." She tried to ignore Ranger's big brown eyes as she lifted a slice to her lips.

"I'll give him something after we're finished." His gaze was steady on her as he waited for her to reply to his command.

She pressed her lips together. "This woman is a housekeeper for somebody named Breckham."

He stiffened.

"You know him," she said in awe.

He gave a nod. "Go on."

She chewed the bite she'd taken and swallowed. "She claims she saw and heard things to make her believe he's involved in dark things. People come to his house, money is exchanged and then they disappear into this big garage on his property. She also said he and his son don't hold back about their dislike for Senator Arthur."

"Breckham is on about five government watch lists. No investigation has ever been able to connect him to crimes, but—"

"I believe he backs those who do his dirty work. He gives them money and gets what he wants in trade."

"Exactly." He wolfed down the rest of his first slice and sipped some water. "I think the best thing for us to do is call the guys over and formulate a plan of action."

She blinked. "The Ranger Ops team, you mean?"

He nodded and reached for his phone.

"Now?" she asked.

He met her gaze. "Yeah, why?"

"It's just that… I'm here. Can you have secret meetings with me in the house?"

He chuckled and thumbed a group text to six numbers. Then he set aside his phone and reached for another slice.

She gaped at him. "Just like that you've ordered a meeting, and you're not even worried about what to say or how to go about things? You just go on eating like it's no big deal."

He shrugged. "It's our jobs. And they will love you. By the way, I told them to grab more pizzas on their way over."

She couldn't possibly eat now — her nerves were too frayed. She was about to meet the men of Lennon's team, and who knew if they'd like her or believe her all wrong for their teammate.

And she *had* told him she was falling for him.

It might have begun as a slow burn, with her denying her interest in the hunky man. She'd avoided his advances and texts, believing she didn't have space in her life for a man right now. Then she'd dragged him smack into the middle of a mess she'd created by attempting to shove herself in her father's face. And now...

She slanted a look at him from beneath her lashes. She thought about walking away from him... and it hurt.

He suddenly threw her a grin that stole her breath. Damn, did the man have to be so gorgeous that her mind turned to mush just from a simple grin?

Knowing her feelings were blossoming caused even more worries, though. He was in a dangerous field of work. She wouldn't know where he was or what he faced. He could be killed.

He set aside his pizza and scooted closer to her around the coffee table. "Hey, you okay? You have a look on your face."

Should she tell him what was on her mind? Wasn't that what couples did?

She pushed out a breath. "I was just thinking about how dangerous your job is."

His face blanked, and then a tender expression took its place. "Baby... I can't promise the future, but I can tell you that today, right here and now, I'm here for you. And I care for you more than you can even know."

She searched his eyes. "Care for?"

He swallowed hard and then said it. "Love. I love you, Edie."

Her emotions rocketed up inside her and spilled over. Tears burned at her eyes, and she crawled the rest of the distance to him. When she pushed him onto his back and kissed him, he brought his arms around her and held her tight.

Looking down into his eyes, she said it too. "I'm falling in love with you too, Lennon. I'm sorry it took me so long to figure out what a great guy you are."

Smile lines appeared around his eyes. "I knew I'd break you down with all my charm."

She pressed her lips to his, and his smile spread beneath it. After that, things got a little heated with Lennon rolling her nipples between his clever fingers and her rubbing against the bulge in his jeans, but a knock at the door pulled them apart.

When she sat up, she looked at the plates on the coffee table. Both were empty. Several feet away, Ranger sat there with his jaws spread into a happy smile.

"Oh Lord," she groaned. "Pizza thief. I'm clearly going to have to watch you better, aren't I?"

"He's fine. I've given him pizza before. But you shouldn't have stolen it, Ranger." He shook a finger at the dog as he made his way to the door to answer it.

She just got to her feet as Lennon swung open the door to reveal the man he'd acknowledged on the street. Her bodyguard.

She felt a flush coat her cheeks. This man had followed her without her knowing, and it felt odd she didn't even know his name.

He walked in carrying two six-packs of beer. Switching both to one hand, he hooked an arm around Lennon, and they delivered a single thump to each other's backs.

Seeing all this testosterone in one space was making her feel like a complete weakling. When they broke apart, the man fixed his gaze on her.

"Hi, Edie."

"Hello." She came forward and held out her hand. "I'm sorry, I don't know your name."

"Penn."

"Thank you for watching out for me."

He gave her a quirk of his lips. Did every rugged manly man give that crooked smile? Maybe there was a course on how to do it. Any woman would be shivering with pleasure at seeing one crooked smile let alone two at once.

"Come in and take a seat. I'll put the beer in the fridge." Lennon walked out of the room, leaving her alone with Penn.

She didn't know what to say to a man who'd probably seen her pick her workout pants out of her butt. "So you're in the Ranger Ops?"

He shook his head. "That's my brother Nash."

"Oh."

"I'm in securities. I go where I'm asked, and I set my own pay scale. These guys are stuck with whatever OFFSUS gives them." He grinned at Lennon as he returned carrying both the chairs from the kitchen set.

"Now I'm more confused. OFFSUS?" Her inner journalist was taking notes as quickly as possible.

"Operation Freedom Flag Southern US division," Lennon said on his way to the entryway. There he plucked up a heavy-looking bench as if it weighed ounces. He carried it back and set it across from the sofa.

Her mind worked over his words. It was shocking how much the common person didn't know about the American government. The fact they were trusting her with this knowledge made her feel closer to Lennon.

He and Penn polished off the pizza, and Edie nibbled on a slice too, since Ranger had eaten what was on her plate. Listening to the guys discuss mundane things — baseball scores, a local craft beer joint that had opened a few miles away — left Edie in wonder. These men protected people with their lives, but they were just ordinary guys.

The knock at the door had Ranger barking and running to it, and Lennon got up to let the rest of the team in. Five chiseled men entered the living room, and suddenly it didn't feel so spacious.

Penn clapped Nash on the back and they bro-hugged. When they did, Edie saw the family resemblance.

When a man identical to Lennon walked in, she sucked in a gasp. She spun to Lennon, and he shot her a grin. "Didn't know I had a twin, I take it."

She shook her head, staring between them. From height to features to mannerisms, he and this man were the same. If she'd come into a room to see him, she would have believed it was Lennon.

"Edie, this is my brother Lincoln."

"I go by Linc." He extended a hand, and she shook it. A closer inspection revealed Linc possessed more scars and some burn marks on his hands too. She watched as the pair embraced, and thought of how proud their momma must be — and what trouble these twins must have given the poor woman in their youth.

The other men crowded in.

Lennon slipped his arm around her waist and pulled her near when he introduced them to her. She locked their names into her mind and said hello.

Edie couldn't help but stare at each of them, as rugged and dangerous as the next. Three pizzas were scattered on the coffee table, and the dog paced back and forth, hoping for a chance to steal more for his supper. The guys dug in and ate like they hadn't had food in weeks.

When the boxes were empty and beers cracked open, Lennon looked at everyone. "We all know why I called this meeting."

They nodded. Edie knotted her fingers, tense.

They were here because of her actions. If she had never gotten up at that speech, she wouldn't be targeted and her father would be on his own. She didn't know whether to feel ashamed or relieved that the senator was finally getting some backup from Ranger Ops.

The man named Jess spoke out. The fierce expression he wore softened as he turned his gaze on her. "I've done some digging and made a connection."

Her heart thumped hard. Did she want to hear this?

"Investigators have dug into the senator's opponents before, looking at their supporters and those who donate campaign money. But I looked into those who support the senator instead."

"Oh no," she whispered. "I suspected something like this."

Lennon, seated next to her on the floor, placed a hand over hers where they twisted in her lap. "What did you find out, Jess?"

"It seems the senator accepted campaign money from an advocacy group. They gave him twenty thousand dollars for his upcoming run for the seat in the Senate."

"What is this group's interest? Gun laws?" she broke in.

Jess tipped his head. "In a way, I guess you could say that. Their interest is vague, at least on the books. Off the record, though, I suspected it could have other ties. Turns out, I'm right."

He pulled out his phone. "The figurehead of the group is Richard Duncan. A nobody, as far as I can see, just a nerd who's into politics. Until you look at his family history and discover his brother is tight with another group, and that one is headed by a George Breckham, Jr."

Her head snapped up. "This information is right there on the surface, yet the authorities haven't discovered it and connected the dots? They've let the attacks continue on my father."

Jess sat back on the sofa and eyed her. "I believe the senator might have known what he was getting into."

"Which is...?" she prompted.

"That the group would have leverage over him."

She swallowed hard. "But their ideas are clearly not on the same track as Senator Arthur's or else they wouldn't attack him and his... family. You think he went into the agreement, and accepted funds from the group, knowing this?"

Jess gave a shrug. "I don't know what was in his mind, but I know fundraising is rough on politicians. A group comes up and hands you a check for twenty grand, you could find yourself influenced."

She shook her head. "I don't believe he would have done something like that. He stands for stricter gun laws while retaining the citizens' right to bear arms. He wouldn't risk his entire platform for money."

"Do you think they tricked him then?" Lennon asked her.

"They might have. But like Jess, I don't know."

Lennon turned her hand over in his, studying her fingers too intently. "If anybody could get in there and ask him, it's you, Edie."

She stared at Lennon in shock. "I'm supposed to just waltz in and ask the senator whether or not he knew he was siding with this group? One that not only didn't have his interests in mind but could be funded by Breckham? And Breckham is a suspected mafia head with links to illegal weapons traders? What good will knowing this do? The senator and his family deserve to be protected. This has to end regardless of whether or not he signed a deal with the Devil."

Lennon gave a nod. "You're right. We're trying to end it... and you going in there to ask could give us the opportunity to steal in from behind. The senator's being watched. You're being watched, Edie."

She jerked her head to look at Penn. He nodded.

Her heart thumped faster.

"So I'm the bait," she said.

"We'll keep you safe." Lennon took hold of her hand and squeezed.

"It's a solid plan." The leader of the group, Nash, but everyone called Sully, eyed them all. "We make it known Edie's going in to speak to the senator. They're both tailed, and we can keep that controlled. Remember, we're in charge of the game. Then once they make their move, we stop it."

She looked into Lennon's eyes. It was a solid plan, wasn't it?

He seemed to hear her mental question and nodded. "I'll be there with you, Edie. I'll protect you with my life."

Her voice wobbled as she said, "That's what I'm afraid of."

Chapter Ten

Lennon had gone over the plan of attack a dozen times just this morning. He walked himself through each step, his focus on keeping Edie safe, and right through to the end result of the Ranger Ops team finally stopping the attacks for good.

Edie hadn't spoken much in the two days since they'd met in his living room and laid out the path. How could he blame her? She wasn't only putting herself on the line. To truly put a stop to the attacks, to give her back her life, she had to rely on the Ranger Ops, which was stressing her.

When she had spoken, it was to tell Lennon that there must be some other way besides him leading the team in there. That she couldn't live with herself if something happened to them.

He drew her onto his lap and held her close. "I know all that. But this is what we do, and you've got to put your trust in us. In me."

She hadn't said more than a dozen sentences since that moment, and he was growing more concerned as the time to roll on the action approached.

Since she was out for a walk with Ranger right now, he was given a chance to touch base with Jess, who was on the intel part of the operation.

Jess walked into the house and closed the door behind him before looking around. "She here?" he asked Lennon.

He shook his head. "Out with the dog. We've got a few minutes to connect with her phone before she comes back."

"Tell me again why you don't want her to know you're doing this? Is this some controlling man thing with you? Making sure your girl doesn't text other guys?" Jess settled at the computer desk in front of Lennon's system, which was up and ready to go.

"Hell no. I trust Edie. But she's already freaked the fuck out. If she knows we're hacking her phone and the senator's in the meantime, she won't want to text. But we both know we need to know what's in his phone—and we can only get into it via hers once we give her the number to text him for the meeting."

Jess nodded. "All right, give it here."

Lennon handed over her phone. It was going behind her back to tap her line, and when it was all over, he planned to tell her about it. She was nervous enough about reaching out to her father and requesting he meet her without knowing everything that was private and personal to the senator was subject to the Ranger Ops team.

Jess took the phone and pressed some buttons. A screen popped up but disappeared in a flash. He handed it back to Lennon.

"That's it?"

"That's it. Everything she texts will be seen on the app I created. And we will have access to everything she connects to, even by brief texts. We could hack the fucking Pentagon with this software, man."

"Let's hope she doesn't have a friend working for the government, then. I don't relish being put behind bars, all from your genius evil." Lennon set her phone back on the coffee table, where she'd left it.

Jess looked at him. "You good, man? You seem stressed."

"I'm fine. Why wouldn't I be?"

"This is your woman we're talking about, not some ordinary mission."

"None of them are ordinary, are they, man?"

Jess chuckled. "Guess you're right. What I'm saying is, you love this woman and everything that happens is going to affect you or her. Which means both of you."

Lennon ran his fingers through his hair. "I got this. I'll be fine. We just need to count down the minutes now."

Jess stood. "I'm off. I'm getting in a date before liftoff."

Lennon followed him to the door and bumped his knuckles against his buddy's. "I'm sure you mean you'll be getting liftoff on this date."

Jess waggled his eyebrows. "You bet your ass I am."

Laughing, Lennon closed the door behind him and glanced back at Edie's phone. It looked exactly the same as before, but now things were different.

He'd gone behind her back.

But it was to ensure her safety, in the end. Anything they had on the senator would help them with their plan to lure in his attackers... the same people the senator had warned Edie to hide from.

Yes, it was the only way, and Lennon couldn't dwell on how many relationship rules he'd just broken.

When she entered the house with a panting Ranger, he came to greet her. Taking the leash from her hand, he disconnected it from the dog and hung it up.

Ranger trotted through the living room to the kitchen. They heard him lapping water.

Edie flashed Lennon a smile that didn't quite reach her eyes. She cocked her head. "Sure he's drinking from his bowl and not the toilet?"

"No, I'm not sure." He laughed. Then he eyed up her body. In a curve-skimming tank top and workout pants, she was sexy as hell.

He moved closer.

"I'm so sweaty, you won't want to touch me," she protested, dodging aside.

He made a grab for her again. She giggled and sidestepped him again.

Finally, he nabbed her around the middle and hauled her up against him. Looking down into her beautiful blue eyes, he rumbled, "Why don't we hit the shower together?"

"Mmm. That sounds pretty nice." She stared at his mouth.

He lowered it to kiss her, the soft brushing of lips making him instantly hard.

Taking her by the hand, he led her through the house to the bathroom. The option of tub or shower gave him pause, but when Edie began to strip, he didn't care what they did as long as she was naked and wet.

Watching her openly, he switched on the water in the shower and gave her a striptease of his own. He tugged his T-shirt out of his cargo pants.

She drew her sports bra up and over her head.

Her candy-hard nipples puckered even further.

He pulled off his own shirt, standing still for her to stare at back. Her gaze zigzagged over his chest to his abs and lower to the bulge growing in his pants.

When she hooked her thumbs into her panties and slowly lowered them over her thighs, exposing her bare mound and her slit beneath it, he let out a hungry growl.

He dropped to his knees, hands planted on her hips. He swayed her a step closer at the same time he opened his mouth. His tongue met her outer lips and sank into her sweet nectar.

She shivered and dug her fingers into his shoulders, rocking her body closer as he slowly lapped up and down her seam. She was soaked and ready for him. And he was hard after only one taste.

The feel of her pussy clenching and releasing on his tongue sent him into overdrive. He pulled back and looked up at her.

She'd bitten her lips into a plumpness that was driving him crazy. "Don't stop, Lennon."

Guiding her to the shower, he placed her inside, dropped the rest of his clothing and joined her. He backed her up against the wall and plunged his tongue into her mouth.

She gasped as she tasted herself and yanked him closer, fingers wrapping around his cock. When she guided him to her bare pussy, he shuddered.

"I forgot a condom," he grated out. "We'll have to play in other ways."

She rewarded him with a sassy smile and dropped to her knees. When she took him into her mouth, he let his head drop back. Water coursed over his spine, but he hardly felt it as her lips closed around him.

* * * * *

The need to pleasure Lennon drove her on. With increasingly stronger pulls of her mouth, she reveled in the sound of his throaty groans. She stole a peek at his face, and her heart swelled with passion and love.

The past day or so had been difficult on her — she hated the entire situation and dragging her lover and his team into it was making her sick to her stomach. But in the end, she had to trust them.

She trusted Lennon with her life... and her heart.

As he let out a rough moan, her inner thighs clenched, and her pussy flooded with desire. The sexy way he looked down at her while she pleasured him gave her a dizzying sensation.

Running her tongue down the side of his shaft and back up to the tip, where she swirled it over the depression, she stared into his eyes.

"Jesus," he gritted out, clamping a hand on her shoulder. He drew her up to her feet and trapped her against the wall of the shower. Holding her gaze prisoner too, he slipped two slick fingers between her legs.

She sucked in a harsh cry of ecstasy as he stroked her clit and then eased his fingers down to her opening. When he drove them in, high and hard, she cried out without restraint.

Need blasted her. For long moments as he finger-fucked her with slow, precise movements, she lost herself. His lips moved across hers, nibbling and biting. He moved to her earlobe and grazed it with his teeth.

He settled the pad of his thumb over her clit and pressed down.

She exploded in a brilliant display of stars behind her eyes. He thrust his tongue into her mouth and dragged her bliss on and on until her knees sagged and he was supporting her against the shower wall.

Before she'd totally come to her senses, she reached for his cock, guiding it to her pussy. "Fuck me, Lennon. I need you."

He went dead still, eyes dark and burning.

"Baby—"

She hitched her thigh around his hip and angled her pussy toward his swollen head. "I'm clean, I'm protected. I've had an IUD for years. Lennon—"

He cut her off, slamming his mouth over hers. The bruising and desperate kiss had her digging her fingers into his shoulders. The tip of his cock brushed her folds, without barriers.

He went still. Tore his mouth free.

"I'm clean, baby. And I've been dying to make you mine since the first time I set eyes on you." With that, he plunged deep into her pussy, half lifting her against the wall to sink right to the base.

Her inner walls clutched at him. He stole her mind with another kiss and withdrew his cock before thrusting back inside. On a whimper, she said, "I love you, Lennon."

"God, woman, you rip me up." He sank deep and began to pulsate, his cock shooting into her, coating her walls with warm cum. The sensation made her pussy squeeze hard, and then she was shaking apart for him too.

The last thing she heard before the final pulsation hit her was, "I love you, Edie. Fuck, I love you."

Somehow the rough declaration was the best in the world.

* * * * *

Lennon was rarely so keyed up before a mission. He went in, did his job and did it well. But this time was different.

It meant putting Edie in danger before they could protect her.

He paced back and forth, shoving his fingers through his hair every four steps. Then he looked at his phone for word from Jess that they had everything set up and ready to roll.

As soon as Edie dialed her father's number that Jess had been able to discover by means of hacking, her texts would ping off cell towers and satellites, making her traceable. Her location would be found, and Jess had done the research on the senator too. His phone wasn't as clean as he and his protective team believed it was.

Lennon issued a sigh.

"Sit down," Linc commanded. "You're driving me crazy with your pacing."

He turned to look at his twin. "If this was Nealy, what would you be doing?"

"Not pacing."

Lennon snorted. "Yeah, you'd be kicking down someone's door and throwing grenades through windows."

Linc glanced up with a grin. "You know me too well, brother."

"When is Jess going to give her the go-ahead to text the senator?"

"Soon. We have a strict timeline. Stick to the plan." Linc hitched his ankle over his opposite knee in a relaxed pose that made Lennon grind his teeth.

The decision had been made to go forward with this plan of attack—but there was still time to back out.

Linc cleared his throat, gaining Lennon's attention. When he looked to his twin, Linc pointed at a chair. "Sit before I break your legs."

Lennon shot his brother a glare but took the seat.

When his phone buzzed seconds later, he leaped up and brought it to his ear. "Jess, whattaya got?"

"You're not gonna like it, Lennon. Something just came through."

"What the fuck is it?"

Linc stood and came closer. Lennon put the phone on speaker so he could hear as well.

Jess continued, "The senator took money from this extremist group knowing full well what he was doing. It's all a hoax, Lennon. He knew the group would attack him. He did it for sympathy votes and publicity."

Lennon blinked. Then his blood ran cold.

Linc grabbed Lennon's shoulder. "Jess, Linc here. If this is the case, the senator put his daughter into danger knowingly."

"Technically, she got on that stage and made herself visible to the group he put himself in the target zone with. But yeah, it's all his doing. They know where he's at 24/7 anyway—our plan isn't going to work to draw them in. They've made a deal with them to get the most for their money. They're going to shoot high—hit the family he has in the public eye, not a secret daughter."

"Fuck!" Lennon scraped his fingers through his hair again, heart rattling hard in his chest. The fury running through him was bigger than anything he'd felt since his twin had been taken.

The fucking senator had entered the agreement with the rebel group knowing he'd be attacked. And he'd done so without regard to his family's safety.

All for the numbers at the voting polls.

He was too infuriated to speak.

"Thanks, Jess. Keep us informed of anything new," Linc said.

Lennon ended the call, and he and Linc stared at each other. "The son of a bitch deserves to be blown up for taking such chances. No wonder the investigations haven't led anywhere substantial— someone must have discovered this already, and that's why nothing's being done."

"All we can do is keep digging for ways to protect Edie."

"What—with WITSEC? No way could she go into protection. I'd never see her again."

"Are you seriously only thinking of yourself right now, man?" Linc gazed at him.

Lennon's shoulders slumped, and he turned away from his brother. "You're right. If she's got to go into the program to protect herself from this group and her stupid father's doing, then that's what she does. It's just... goddammit, I love her."

Linc bowed his head. "I knew you did."

Lennon didn't think the moment could get much darker after hearing the senator had basically set himself up for the attacks, but this was it. Knowing he'd have to give Edie up in order to keep her safe and alive was ripping his heart out of his chest.

"You've gotta call her and at least tell her about what Jess found," Linc said.

He still could find a way to disconnect her from the senator — a fake DNA test or something — and put it out to the press.

"Lennon." Linc's voice interrupted his thoughts. "Call her and get it over with."

Drawing a deep breath, he nodded. What he was about to tell her would tarnish any decent opinion she had about the senator.

There was no choice.

He walked away from his twin, phone in hand. A second later, he heard Linc go out and the soft click of the door closing.

When he dialed Edie, he flinched at the worry in her tone.

"Lennon, I don't know if I can go through with this."

He pinched the bridge of his nose. "You won't have to. It seems we have an issue."

"What is it?"

He drew a deep breath and exhaled. "The senator took that campaign money knowing he'd become a target. He did this to himself, for votes, Edie."

Silence.

It went on so long, he ached to think of what she must be feeling right now.

"Edie."

"You're saying my father put himself in danger so he could gain public sympathy and more votes?"

"It seems that way. Jess uncovered something."

"I'd like to know what that is. Can you find out for me?" she asked in a stronger tone.

He was proud of her character and ability to move forward even in the face of shock and fear. "Of course."

"So it won't matter if I call the senator. These people probably have attacks planned out weeks beforehand—and the senator might even know of them and be prepared."

"God, I hate to say it, but it could be the case, yes."

"I'm so stupid for getting on that stage," she said softly.

"Baby, you can't go back, only forward."

"Yeah, now I know that I can't have a relationship with my father, never did and never could."

"Edie, I'm sorry. You know you've got me. We'll create our own family. My momma will adore you, and Linc already does."

When her voice came through into his ear, it was thick with emotion. "You're the best, Lennon. I'll talk to you later when you get home, okay? I'm going to take Ranger for a walk and clear my head."

* * * * *

Edie kissed the dog's head and rubbed his ears. As soon as her tears started to fall, Ranger had

202

planted himself in front of her and hadn't budged since. He stared at her with baleful eyes, as if he felt everything she did.

"I'm all right now, boy. Want to go for a walk?"

His ears perked forward at the word, and he jumped to his feet. She followed him as he ran to the door and put on her shoes. When she hooked the leash to his collar, he gave an excited leap.

It was impossible not to chuckle at his antics, and that made her feel better. She went out and set the alarm system. Before she stepped onto the sidewalk, Jordan was calling out to her and waving.

"I'll be by tomorrow to mow the lawn!" he called.

"Sounds good, thanks," she returned and continued walking, Ranger in the lead.

The ache in her heart made her footsteps slower than usual, and she had to give the dog a command so he didn't pull her down the street.

Her father... how greasy could he get? She knew politicians were often swayed to dirty acts in order to reach the top, but she'd never believed it of Senator Arthur.

What had her mother seen in the man? Edie could chalk the affair up to the stupidity of a young woman with stars in her eyes as she followed him around the campaign circuit. But had he been so crazed for success that he didn't care how he climbed the rungs of the ladder even back then?

It was a question she'd never have answered. It was best to let go of any thoughts of the senator in relation to herself — they were too different. She never would have put people she loved into danger the way he had.

Then she'd added herself to the target list. How was she going to get herself out of this mire?

Knowing she had Penn to watch her back gave her the freedom to think — and mentally rage. The anger hit hard and hot, leaving her stomping down the sidewalk, practically dragging Ranger now.

Her breaths came faster, and she tried to slow her steps. Killing herself walking the dog in the Texas heat wouldn't do her any good in the end. She had to keep a level head.

In her mind, she listed the things she did have — Lennon and his team prepared to keep her safe. But she couldn't continue to live this way, with Penn following her every time she set foot outside and keeping to the shadows outside Lennon's home in case somebody tried to breach it.

She had Hallie. Her friend would do anything in her power to help her, and Edie could use more help digging into what she'd learned about the senator from Lennon.

She also had her own wits. She'd clawed her way up before, and she would now. She would get her life back.

As she and Ranger turned another corner on the stretch for home, an idea began to form in her head... It just might work.

But Lennon wouldn't like it one bit.

Chapter Eleven

Lennon grabbed his Kevlar and slipped it over his chest. The rest of the team was in similar stages of putting on their gear. Being on standby sucked in the best of times, but with so much weighing on Lennon's mind, he'd rather be anywhere else.

"This is bad timing," he muttered to Jess at his left.

"Is there ever a good time?" The man had stress creases between his brows and extending up into his forehead.

Lennon looked at him closer. "You good, man?"

Jess sank to the bench to lace up his combat boots. "Never better."

"Sure sounds like it. What's up? More woman troubles?"

"I wish. It's some new intel OFFSUS has me working on. Listening to terrorists and cartel at all hours of the day is getting pretty fucking old."

"It's gotta weigh on you, hearing all that shit and dissecting it into something real. Just keep taking the breaks you need—stay centered on what's going on in your own life. It's the only way to process that shit."

It was a known fact that military intelligence officers got into dark places. You couldn't very well listen into plans to torture humans and not lose a little humanity yourself. Hearing that shit made a man want to grab a fucking machine gun and wipe out everybody involved.

"Talk to the team counselor too. Don't let it overcome you, Jess."

"I'll be good." The man tugged hard on his boot lace without looking up.

Lennon watched him another second before returning to his gear.

Linc walked over and leaned against the locker, watching.

"Need somethin'?" Lennon asked.

"Wondered if you might. I know this morning wasn't easy for you, after learning that shit about the senator."

He blew out a sigh. "I've had better moments. But I'm good."

"And Edie?"

"She's all right, I think."

"Tough break, us getting put on standby and you can't go home and talk things out with her."

He looked up at his twin. If anyone understood how Lennon was feeling right now, it was Linc. He nodded. "I wish I had some time, that's for sure. That's the downfall of having this gig and working around a family. I'm seeing that now."

"Yeah, but it's not so bad. Don't let it deter you. Nealy and I make it work. Same with the others." He did a chin-lift toward the rest of the guys at their lockers, strapping on their gear.

At that moment, Sully and Shaw laughed at something Cav said. Lennon found himself smiling too without even knowing what they were laughing over. The team was a constant for him—they had his back and he had theirs. They were family he chose, a brotherhood.

No matter what happened with Senator Arthur, the Ranger Ops would remain the same. What he wasn't so sure of was... would Edie?

She was affected by that man's choices in life, and it couldn't feel good to be tossed out by her own father, reminded of it again after all these years of no contact.

On the top shelf of his locker, Lennon's phone buzzed as a call came in. He snatched the cell and brought it to his ear, hoping it was Edie.

Penn's voice reached him. "Dude, your l'il girl needs another spankin'."

Lennon's heart jerked. "What now?"

"She's visiting the senator."

"Jesus Christ!" He shoved his fingers through his hair. Up and down the lockers, all eyes were on him. "Can you stop her? It's not as if she doesn't know you're following her."

"I tried to talk sense into her, but she threw me a look that would shrivel up a man's balls and make it so he can't father children. Then she pushed by me and walked right into his office."

"Where are you right now?"

"Outside waiting. They won't let me in. Guess I look threatening or some shit," Penn drawled.

"Fuck—we need her outta there, but my hands are tied. You know I'm on standby, right?"

"No, I didn't. You do what you gotta. I'll take care of her."

"Goddammit. I need to be there. What do you think she's doing?" Even as he asked it, he already knew—Edie was confronting the senator.

And by going there, she was visible.

To everyone who could hurt her.

"Sully," he called out, holding the phone away from his ear.

Their leader swung his gaze toward him.

"What the fuck's happening here? Are we goin' in or what?"

"Haven't heard anything in the last five minutes. Let me hit up the colonel again."

Lennon brought the phone back to his ear. "Penn, get her out of there."

"Copy."

The line went dead, and Lennon slammed a fist into the locker. The pain traveled up his arm as the metal vibrated from the blow.

Sully walked over. "What's going on?" he asked, low.

"Goddammit, my hands are tied." Lennon twisted away, and Sully hooked an arm around his neck, holding him.

"They're never tied. There's always a way. Tell me what's happening."

"Edie's in with the senator. Anything could go down. The cops are worthless in this. It's gotta be us, Sully."

Their gazes met. Suddenly, Sully grabbed his phone and brought it to his ear.

"Colonel Downs, something just came up. We need to know if we're free to take care of it." As he spoke the words, he stared at Lennon.

He gave Lennon a small nod and thanked the Colonel.

"Time to roll out, boys. We're paying a visit to the senator." Lennon swung toward the door.

I'm coming, Edie. God, don't do anything rash.

* * * * *

"Senator Arthur has cancelled his meeting and agreed to meet you." The receptionist stood before

Edie with a small smile in place. Did the woman know who she was? Did Edie give a damn?

Straightening her shoulders, she followed the woman into a spacious office. Edie threw a look around, but the senator wasn't here yet.

"He'll be right in. He told me to ask you to wait." She smiled at Edie, but her gaze traveled over her features and upward to encompass her hair.

Yeah, she was recognizable, the resemblance uncanny if you put them side by side or knew the senator's face well enough, which this woman would.

"Thank you," she said quietly. Her heart thumped harder, faster, louder. The receptionist closed the door, and Edie walked up to the chairs in front of the desk. Rather than take a seat, she circled the heavy wooden desk and stared at the personal items on it.

Expensive items. No Chinese junk here. It was all real leather or heavy brass. Her gaze landed on a silver frame containing a photo of the senator and his family.

A lump wedged in her throat, and she had to swallow hard around it. Looking at the faces of his kids—her own half-siblings—was surreal. This was the closest she'd ever come to them.

Both bearing the brown hair of their mother as well as her face shape and the color of her eyes, they were far from the senator.

211

A footstep made her jerk. She glanced up to fix her gaze onto the senator.

Her father.

For the second time seeing him, she felt pretty collected even if tongue-tied.

She set the frame back in its place and moved around the desk. "Senator."

He closed his eyes briefly and opened them again. This time his eyes were shining with emotion.

"I'm so glad to see you in one piece, Eden — Edie. But why did you take a risk in coming here?"

He wore a business suit as usual, and she felt very underdressed in her jeans and top, the classiest items she had with her at Lennon's house.

"I had to see you."

He seemed to be restraining himself from speaking. Finally, he nodded and gestured to a chair.

She sat and faced him across the desk. "I know about you accepting campaign money from the group targeting you. I know that it's all a ploy for you to get voters' sympathy."

Her words must have been like a slap across the face — he reared back in shock.

"Edie. For God's sake, you can't believe I'm that sort of man."

"I don't know what you are. I don't know you."

"Christ," he said softly, rumpling his sleek, perfect hair with his fingers. "That's what they want everyone to believe. This is what they're trying to do, Edie. They're undermining all my claims of the attacks. They've done this before... with that senator in Ohio."

Her stare bored into his. "Tell me what you mean." Her voice took on one of command.

The senator drew up and leaned forward, hands on his desk. For the first time, she saw she also shared the shape of his fingers and fingernails. Her mind spun out on this revelation. She was seeing a parent that gave her up and making all the connections to him, things she'd wondered about herself for her entire life.

"The group got to the senator in Ohio some years back. Gave him funds but under false pretenses — the same terms they presented to me. Had I known what they really were, I never would have accepted that check. I would have shredded it to pieces. But I didn't know. The things they promised involved my backing, that they wanted gun laws put into effect as much as I did."

"Go on." She didn't want to see the desperate light in his eyes or feel the pang of sympathy she did.

"Once the check was signed and the deposit made, they came back to me, told me that now they owned me."

She didn't blink, listening intently to his story while searching him for signs of dishonesty.

"They started making demands. That I change my stance on the gun laws. That I side for no more laws and lesser restrictions on weapons. That the prison sentences for illegal arms dealers be lowered."

She issued a slow breath, taking it all in, but said nothing.

"Edie." He pushed to his feet and came around the desk to sit next to her. "This group is terrorizing all of us. You have to believe me when I say I did not sign up for this in order to get more voters' support. When they did the same thing to the politician in Ohio, he spoke out and they discredited him. They put it out into the media that he had been staging the attacks. Of course, only a day passed before he was out of the running. *This is what they want from me.* I've resisted thus far. It hasn't been easy." The vehemence in his voice was the same passionate tone that had people following him, her included.

But it did not sound like a guilty man either.

"Please believe me. I know you think badly of me already, and I don't blame you. I could have accepted the heat from your birth years ago, and I didn't. I was afraid and... cowardly." His blue eyes, just like hers, swam with tears. "I'm sorry for all of it. If I had it to do over, I'd never make the same mistake. You'd be in that photo with us, Edie." He waved toward the photo on his desk.

She dropped her head, unwilling to show him the emotion on her own face... that looked just like his.

"Please don't believe them. It's what they want from you, from everybody. I've made mistakes in my life, but I would never do awful things — atrocities — to those I love." Reaching out, he skimmed a thumb across her cheek.

Tears spilled over the rims of her eyes and tumbled down her cheeks. "You don't have to claim to love me."

"But I do." The passion was back in his tone, and it raised gooseflesh on her arms. "How can I have a child out there in the world that I don't love? I always have. But I've been wrong in allowing so many years to pass, Edie."

She looked into his eyes and saw genuineness that struck her to the core.

"I'll tell my wife. I'll tell my kids they have a sister."

She pulled away from his touch. "It's not necessary to ruin your relationships. I've lived without you this long."

He looked stricken for a moment, but it was replaced by awe. "I admire you, Edie. You're strong like your mother."

She believed everything he'd just told her. Now she could move forward.

She opened her mouth to speak and was cut off by a blast. An explosion that rocked the building.

Her father threw himself at her. She hit the floor with a smack, which knocked the wind out of her, and she curled onto her side like a bug, gasping for breath and trying to find reason.

"Stay down!" Her father hovered over her, shielding her with his body as a second explosion hit. *An uncaring man wouldn't do that.*

In the back of her mind, she called out to Lennon.

* * * * *

Smoke wafted up all around Lennon, and a roar collected in his throat. He couldn't even make out what was ahead of him, but he was looking for a fucking door—the door leading to Senator Arthur's office.

To Edie.

"I can't get a view. It's filled with smoke." Linc's voice projected through his comms unit.

"Me either. Goddammit!"

There was no holding back.

"I'm going in."

He took a Hail Mary step forward that could cost him his life if the floor collapsed from beneath him. After the back-to-back explosions, anything was possible, and he'd seen a lot of bad shit go down in situations like this.

Finding Edie was worth any risk. She had to be alive. He had to take her home to his momma, back to Ranger.

His boot didn't fall through a hole, so he chanced another step. In a crouch to remain under the smoke, he pushed through. His weapon in hand hit something hard, and he came to a stop, finding a wall.

"Lennon, where the hell are you? You can't split off!" Linc's incensed tone held more than anger. Fear tinged it as well.

Lennon couldn't think about that now. "I'm all right. I'm heading toward the office."

"The office was the target—you have no idea if there even *is* an office!" Linc burst out.

"There's gotta be. She's gotta be alive, and I'm going to find her." The smoke was filling the space, but no fire licked up the walls yet. He suspected it was in the floors below, and some of the Ranger Ops were down there now checking it out. They had just breached the building when the first explosion hit. Then the second had come out of nowhere.

He wouldn't be shocked if there were more to come, but the calm part of himself said he must continue on regardless of the risk.

I have to reach you. I'm coming, Edie.

His heart was a constant drum in his ears.

"Goddammit, Lennon. Stop where you are. You're not going without me." Linc's fury made his voice shaky.

"I've stopped. Get your ass up here—now."

Shouts and commands from other members of the team volleyed back and forth as they discovered the root of the smoke, a blaze on the second floor of the building. Fire crews were already inside and were evacuating survivors.

Jesus Christ, was the rebel group proving they could take out the senator and his secret daughter in one strike, or had the attack been planned even before Edie set foot in the building?

Linc's voice filled his ear again. "I've got eyes on you. I should break your nose for splitting off from me, you son of a bitch."

Lennon grunted. "Like to see ya try. Let's go."

Together, they felt their way into the space, crouched beneath the worst of the smoke but still blind. He didn't see the wall until it loomed up before him.

He had a mental map of the building he'd memorized in the days before they planned to set Edie as a decoy, and he knew this wall was the one before the senator's main office. The receptionist should be right behind it.

He entered the space and felt the door. It wasn't hot, but smoke trickled from beneath it, licking and curling upward. If they all weren't dead from smoke inhalation, they'd be damn lucky. He had his mask in place, and they each carried a spare.

Running his hand along the door, he found the handle and flicked the lever downward. Smoke poured out.

"Edie!"

"Fuck," Linc said from behind him.

He turned to see his brother had barreled right into what was probably the secretary, and she'd collapsed before she could reach the door.

"Take care of her. I'm going for Edie," Lennon called out.

Not waiting for his brother's agreement, he charged in. With all the smoke, the things that had fallen off the walls and furniture tossed in the explosion, finding her wouldn't be easy.

He scanned the floor for her.

When he reached another door, he kicked it inward. "Edie!" He bellowed till his vocal cords shook.

"Oh my God! Lennon! Here!"

His heart gave a hard jolt, and he jerked into action. Getting to her took too many seconds, shoving through things that had been heaved over.

The moment he laid eyes on her and the senator, bent over her as if to protect her, Lennon knew he had the man to thank for keeping her safe until Lennon could reach her.

He grabbed her face and looked into her eyes. "Take this." He ripped off his own mask and put it over her face. Above it, her eyes were very blue, red-rimmed from crying.

Reaching into his pack, he came out with the backup mask. "Here." He thrust it into the senator's hands. The gas mask filtered enough air to protect and provide purer oxygen, something they both needed and Lennon could survive without until Linc reached him with his backup mask.

"Are you hurt?" he asked Edie.

She shook her head. The chairs in the room were flipped and a filing cabinet had crashed to the ground.

"We have to get out. The building could collapse," he said. "I need you both to stay down and hold onto each other, make a chain. I'm getting you out."

Moving was slow, and in the hallway outside the office they found Linc. He was hoisting the receptionist over his shoulder. At that moment, firefighters burst into the space, and relief surged through Lennon.

They took the receptionist off Linc's hands and provided Lennon with a mask.

"We'll take her," one said to Lennon, pointing to Edie.

He shook his head. "She's with me. Him too." Ranger Ops had to protect Senator Arthur.

The firefighters asked if anyone else was in that office, and Arthur told them no, that his assistant was elsewhere in the building at the time of the explosion.

Edie's eyes widened. "Jake! Jake is somewhere in the building!"

Her ex-boyfriend. They'd discovered he hadn't been fired with the rest of Arthur's team.

Lennon nodded. "They'll find him. C'mon."

With them forming a chain again, and Linc bringing up the rear behind the senator, they made painstaking progress out of the office and found the stairwell. Lennon took one look at it and saw that the explosion had crushed the foundation beneath the building in this area, making the stairs too perilous to use.

"Find another way," he called to Linc.

"We fucking found the source of the explosion. Two delivery crates on the ground floor. Fucking residue all over the place down here," Cav bit out through the comms.

"Search for more. Look for the assailants too." That from Sully.

"What we need is eyes on Breckham," Lennon said.

Edie turned her head to pierce him with a hard look.

He grasped her arm, heart flexing at the feel of her warm skin even through his glove, and towed her along to the opposite end of the building where the staircase could be still intact.

"Fuckers didn't do a very good job. They thought those two little bombs would take down the building? We might be sitting cockeyed, but we're definitely not collapsing." Cav's words reached them all.

"Yet." Sully's harsh word gave Lennon an instant image of 9-11 in his head and what had happened to those buildings.

This wasn't nearly as tall. The bombs had been small potatoes compared to those jets striking the twin towers. But it made his blood run cold.

The urge to get Edie out and safe burned through him, leaving him sweating like he'd just run through a wall of fire.

From the corner of his eye, he caught Linc's hand signal.

People on the move. Headed toward them.

He shoved Edie into the corner and pressed his back to her. Linc had the senator down and out of sight. In this side of the building, the smoke wasn't nearly as thick, and he made out the backs of two men who were coming from the good stairwell.

They were moving toward the senator's office rapid speed.

Edie's fingers dug into his spine, and he reached back to squeeze her knee.

He got a good ID on the men. They had no firefighters' gear, and they sure as hell weren't Ranger Ops.

When he spotted a weapon in one's hand, he raised his weapon and locked eyes with Linc. They'd done this before.

When the men turned, Lennon gave a small nod and then he and Linc took the shots.

* * * * *

Edie sat in the back of an ambulance being treated for smoke inhalation. The senator had been taken to a more secure area by Penn, and she wondered what would become of the very short moment when she'd felt a father-daughter bond.

"I think I'm all right," she said to the EMT.

"Let me get one more read on your oxygen levels and then you'll be free to go," he said.

She nodded, and he placed a device on her index finger. A beep occurred almost instantaneously, and he gave a nod.

"You're back to normal. Be careful out there, though, okay? There's a lot of traffic with the medics and firetrucks."

Not to mention the special ops team that had rushed in and saved so many.

After thanking the medic, she wandered the immediate area in search of Lennon. He was nowhere to be seen. Without anything to do to help, she found a place out of the way and leaned against a vehicle.

With her legs in such a shaky state, she wished she had a bench or something to sit on. But this would do for now. She pulled out her phone and texted her mother and then Hallie. She owed it to both women who loved her to let them know she was safe, even though they had no idea she'd been in danger.

223

Her mind still whirled over everything that had happened—facing down her father, learning the truth, his vow to tell his family and her refusal of it. Then the explosion that had rocked the building not once but twice. The smoke filling the space had stunned her at first, and then she'd grown furious, realizing the sprinkler system had failed to come on and that it had been shut down—if they hadn't been killed by the blasts, they would be by the fire.

Each time she thought of what might have really happened to her, she wanted to get up and run into the burning building with a grenade launcher to look for the men who'd done this to her.

Was this how Lennon felt?

The look on his face when he'd found her...

Her heart gave a hard knock in her chest.

Hallie's reply came at once, and her eyes blurred with tears as she read her friend's gushing words about how much she loved her and was happy she was safe. Then Hallie told her she was coming for a visit ASAP. That had Edie chuckling through her tears.

Strong arms came around her. She looked up into Lennon's hazel eyes.

"Oh baby." He dragged her flush against his chest, both arms locking her into his embrace. He bowed his nose to her hair. "It's all right. I've got you."

She sniffled and breathed him in... smoke and man with an underlying note of his bodywash.

She held fast to him, finding him bulkier with all the gear he wore. She'd never seen him in full rig, and given other circumstances, she'd want to look her fill.

"Where is the senator?"

"He's safe, his injuries being tended."

"He's injured?"

"Yeah, he crawled through some glass while we were making our escape."

Suddenly, she replayed the sound of those two shots ringing out... the finality of them. Being hidden behind Lennon's big body, she had been unable to see the bullets that had taken out their attackers. But her father had screamed.

"I'll have to get in touch with him and thank him for all he did for me." She shivered, and Lennon enfolded her more tightly in his hold.

"Yes, there is time to say things. I'll get you access as soon as I can. Right now, the guys are wrapping up here, and the building's being double-checked."

"Did..." She could barely speak the words. "Did anybody die?"

"No casualties," he said at once. "Just lots of injuries. One woman on the ground floor nearest the bombs is in critical condition."

"How horrible."

He nodded. "Jake's okay."

"I'm glad. You know I don't care about him... I just hate to see him lose his life—for anybody to lose his life—because of something like this."

He smoothed a hand down her arm. "I understand." He looked at her for a long, silent moment.

"What is it?" she asked, heart starting to pick up pace.

"I shouldn't be telling you this, but the unofficial word is that while we were in there"—he raised his jaw toward the building—"Breckham's home was invaded, and he's been taken into custody."

She sucked in a gasp. "Will it end if he isn't able to call the shots anymore?"

"We'll end it. We don't fuck around." His teeth flashed white in his dark face paint.

She wrapped her arms around his neck and held him. "Thank God you were there, Lennon. How did you get there so quick?"

"We're the Ranger Ops, baby. Guts and glory."

She pushed back to search his eyes. "Guts and glory and a gorgeous man that I love."

"Hey, that better be me."

Disregarding the streaks of his face paint, she yanked him in for a kiss. "There's no one else for me."

* * * * *

226

Edie pushed open the door of her apartment. The familiar scents of home, though stale, were intact.

Penn stepped up. "May I?"

She waved a hand for him to go ahead and do his duty. Though the past two weeks had seen the entire Breckham clan and every person associated with his affairs in custody, Lennon still wasn't taking chances and had kept Penn on as her bodyguard.

He moved through the place, hand on his spine, ready to pull his weapon. She stood there waiting for him to finish and give her the all-clear.

A minute later he was back, a half grin on his face. "You're good. I'll wait outside for you."

"Thanks, Penn."

He strolled to the door, boots thumping on the floor.

She spun. "Penn."

He turned to look at her.

"You don't have to babysit me anymore. I'm safe now and have been for weeks." She'd returned to work even, though it had been a wrench for her to leave Ranger, if she was honest. The new dog sitter she and Lennon had chosen together came with excellent references, was very attentive and lived only a block away from him. She had seen Ranger on walks before and stopped to pet him every chance she got.

But that brief and odd part of Edie's life hadn't been all terror-filled.

She had made friends. With a dog, with Penn... and she had Lennon.

Penn's grin widened into the real deal. "I know you're fine. But tell that to your boyfriend."

"I'll speak to him tonight." She smiled back. "Thank you."

He shot her an affectionate wink and walked out of the apartment.

She closed the door behind him and leaned on it heavily. Looking around the place she had loved when she chose it and decorated it, she felt far removed now. How strange a few weeks with Lennon had changed her universe.

There were things to think about.

To stay here at the apartment or move in with Lennon on a permanent basis? She knew what he wanted already, but it was a decision that she must put some major thought into. After all, jumping into situations had caused all this mess in the first place.

The commute to *Notable News* would be killer, but she was hoping to work out some deal with her editor to work from home some days and email articles for consideration, as she had the write-up on Jordan and school lunches.

A big part of her feared that by staying here in her apartment, she'd allow that cold, unemotional portion of herself to creep back in and she would be distanced from the man she loved.

She couldn't allow that to happen.

There was also the possibility of taking Hallie up on her offer to run her e-zine from a satellite office with weekly meetings in the country and leave behind her dreams of being a full-time reporter with *Notable News.*

Too many options, all the paths leading from what she knew.

She gathered a few things into a suitcase and wheeled it out the door. Expecting Penn to be standing guard, she was shocked to look up into Lennon's eyes.

Arms folded, he pulled away from the wall and sauntered over to stand before her. His expression changed as he saw hers.

"You okay, baby?" he asked, cupping her face.

She nodded. "I think I need a few days to think on things."

Fear struck his eyes like green-gold bolts of lightning. "Think on us," he grated out.

She nodded, eyes downcast. She couldn't face the look she'd put in his eyes. "I love you, Lennon. That much I know. I'm just not sure how to sort everything out—to combine my old life with a new one. And that new one only came about from a mess with the senator—my father." She sighed. "Well, it's a completely different life from what it was. I can't keep up with all the changes."

He slid his hands to her shoulders and kneaded at the tension there. "It's understandable. You've been

229

shaken up and need to find your groove. I'll be here to support you... or back off. If you need." He swallowed hard.

She put her arms around him and rested her head on his shoulder. "I don't want you to back off. But I might need to do some investigation into my own life story. I need to see if I belong at *Notable News*. Climbing that ladder past all the interns who were there before me will take a long time, and I'm not certain anymore if I'm up for that sort of news reporting."

He arched a brow. "You'll go to Hallie?"

She nodded. "I'm still thinking on things there, but I want to visit her."

He shot her a smile. "Sure you can navigate all those farm roads?"

She chuckled. "Yes."

"Here's what I think you should do," he said, taking up the handle of her wheeled suitcase. "You pack up for the country. Spend some time with Hallie talking things out. Then if I'm open this weekend, I'll come join you, and you can meet my momma. But there's no pressure. It's just a suggestion. The last thing I want is to force myself and this life on you, Edie. I'm..." He searched her eyes and started again. "I'm deep in love with you, but your happiness is first and foremost to me. If it means giving you—"

She didn't let him finish his sentence, whatever it was. She went on tiptoe and crushed her lips over his.

The soft lingering brush of his mouth sent tingles all through her body. When she drew away to stare up into his eyes, she smiled. "You're the best boyfriend a girl could ask for. I'll follow your plan and go visit Hallie. Then I'll see you on the weekend. Okay?"

He brought her close and pressed a light kiss to her forehead. "Perfect."

They remained in each other's embrace for a moment.

"I'll leave from here," she said.

"Ranger and I will be waiting for you at my momma's barring I don't get called away."

She grinned and laid a palm on his chest. "Will you do something else for me?"

"Anything, baby." His tone was filled with the love she saw reflected in his eyes.

She tapped his chest. "Take Penn with you."

Epilogue

6 months later

Ranger romped through the back yard, chasing the ball that Lennon lazily whipped out there for him to fetch. For now, holding down the lounge chair was his only chore. That and getting his beautiful woman into his bed again soon.

Edie curled up next to him on the chair, her head resting on his shoulder. The tendrils of her blonde hair spread across his chest, and he stroked the silken strands over and over.

"Ranger's back," she said with a giggle.

The dog stood next to Lennon's chair, ball in his smiling jaws and drool soaking it.

"Give," Lennon said.

The ball dropped into his hand.

"Good boy." He tossed it, and Ranger took off, knocking into the lounger with such force that they were shaken up.

Edie lifted her head off his chest to watch the dog wheel out through the yard and collect the ball. "Where does he find all that energy?" she asked.

"You'd have some too if you hadn't stayed up all night." He stroked his hand down her spine to the curve of her ass.

She wiggled closer. "Whose fault was that, now?"

"You started it," he said.

She had. After several days away on a dark mission, he'd walked through his front door to find Edie sprawled on his sofa, completely naked. As he'd growled out a greeting, she let her thighs part ever so slightly, giving him a view of what he'd been hungering for during their days apart.

Things had gone up in flames in a hurry, and they'd barely rolled away from each other long enough to eat. Actually, if it hadn't been for Ranger bringing them his food bowl, they might still be there in bed.

She arched, filling his palm with her round ass cheek, and looked up into his eyes. "We'd better get on the road if we're making it to the country this evening."

"I'm thinking tomorrow morning is soon enough. Can your meeting with Hallie wait till then?"

"Yes. Would give you time to mow the lawn too." She turned her head to eye the grass. Since school was back in session, Jordan was busy, and happily getting school lunches again since Edie's story in *Notable News* had sent other parents like Jordan's into action. Together they'd been able to fundraise enough money to give each child a free lunch for half of the school year. Their efforts continued, and they hoped to make that the entire year by the time they were finished.

Edie's backside vibrated, and Lennon paused in groping it.

"Want me to get that for you?" He cocked a brow.

"Yes, please."

He drew her phone out nice and slow, teasing her, before handing it over.

She looked at the screen and pushed up a little more, surprise crossing her face.

"My father's invited us to join them all in Colorado for the New Year."

This was the most surprising of all the things to have happened to Edie so far, at least in Lennon's opinion. Her father actually had broken the news to his family. It had sent Edie into a tizzy for a while, and no wonder. He couldn't imagine how it would feel to be the daughter nobody knew about. Would they all resent her?

Turned out, their issues with how she had come into the senator's life didn't last for long. Her half brother and sister were slowly reaching out, and she and Lennon had shared dinner with the Arthurs twice now.

"Christmas Eve with your mother here," he said.

"And Christmas Day with yours," she added.

"A long weekend in the country. Linc and Nealy will be there." Linc had told him they had news to share, and Lennon thought he could guess what it was. Nealy had been looking very green for a couple months and now suddenly appeared radiant and glowing.

"And New Years with the Arthurs in Colorado?" She looked into Lennon's eyes.

He nodded. "I haven't skied in years. I can't break anything, or I won't be with Ranger Ops for six weeks after."

She ran her hand down his chest to the waistband of the lounge pants he'd thrown on after their sex marathon. "I think I know a way to keep you off the slopes..."

He grabbed her ass and hauled her over him, his cock already growing hard between her thighs. "Sounds like one hell of a holiday," he said.

She leaned in to kiss him. In seconds, their tongues twined and heat blazed through him.

Suddenly, a slobbery ball dropped onto his chest.

Edie collapsed into giggles. "Ranger's back."

"We need to figure out a way to tire this dog out so we can get more alone time together."

"I know. Why don't we take him for a walk? Right after this." She kissed him again.

The love and need in her caress extended deep into him, and he gave it right back, matching the love of his life... stroke for stroke.

THE END

Read on for a sneak peek of TARGET IN RANGE

The wind howled through the trees outside Avery's bedroom window, but it didn't mask the thump of boots and slamming of doors.

Somebody was in the house.

Why, oh why had she said she was too old for a babysitter? Her parents wouldn't be home for hours from their cards night with friends, and she knew those rough, low voices coming from the front of the house were not her parents.

She had woken the second she heard the back door. Nobody used the back, and from that moment, she knew what was going on.

Robbers had come, and she was alone. Helpless.

Her heart pounded in her ears and filled her chest, slamming until it hurt and she felt it all the way up into her teeth. Her hands were icy, but there was no turning over and cuddling beneath her Hello Kitty quilts.

She had to hide.

The men weren't bothering to be quiet—they thought the house was empty. They were coming toward her bedroom.

"Find the bedroom. Women always have jewelry." One man's voice jolted as with how close it was to her door.

"Might be a gun there too."

"Yeah, gotta protect against people like you."

The coarse words barely registered in Avery's head. She rolled out of bed to her knees. Thank goodness she had carpet and made no sound. But she couldn't move either—she was frozen in fear, stare locked on the door, waiting for it to burst inward and the evil men looking her in the eyes.

She peered through the strands of her brown hair. They wavered in front of her vision, because she was shaking.

One more heavy footstep, just outside her door. She scrambled up and lunged toward her closet.

No, it was always the first place robbers looked. She needed another hiding spot.

Avery was a reader, and for her tenth birthday, her daddy had construction workers come in and build her a book nook around her window with a seat underneath. Her momma had sewn her a plump cushion, and Avery spent hours curled up there reading every chance she got.

Shelves surrounded the window, all packed with her favorite mysteries and books about girls winning championships for riding horses. Recently, her teacher had loaned her the first book of a series about girls in middle school, and Avery was captivated by all the changes that would take place in her future, namely getting boobs and liking boys.

Under the window seat was an empty space, not yet filled with books, but Avery had shoved some old sneakers in there when her momma told her to clean her room. The space was big enough to hide in.

Shuffling on hands and knees as fast as she could, she reached the cupboard and yanked it open. Diving inside head-first, she held her breath. Her lungs burned and her head swam. She took a shallow breath and let it trickle out slowly as she drew the door shut.

Too late, she realized she might not be able to open the cupboard door from the inside and could be trapped in here without much air and a pair of dirty old sneakers stuffed in the corner until her parents came home.

In her parents' room, she heard drawers opening and things hitting the floor as they were tossed about. Ransacked, was the word, she'd read once. Until now, she hadn't totally understood its meaning.

Pressing a hand over her drumming heart, she strained to listen. She heard a lamp smash, probably the pretty one with flowers her momma liked so much. And then one man said, "Found it."

"Looks like a .38 Special."

"Yeah, bullets too. Now find the jewelry and we can get outta here."

Avery slumped in the cupboard, nose smashed against the wood bottom while tears silently rolled down her cheeks. *Please don't let my mom and dad come home till they're gone. Please don't' let them come for me too.*

When the steps moved out of her parents' room next door to hers, she squeezed her eyes shut and mentally begged them not to come in. Her door burst inward, smashing off the wall.

"Just a kid's room. Nothin' here."

The steps moved on.

She focused on the sound of them moving through the rest of the house and finally heard nothing. Her heart wouldn't slow, and she was terrified to open the cupboard door to find the men staring at her, so she stayed hidden until she heard her father's shouts and her mother's shrill cry.

"Avery!"

It was a long time before she could sleep in her own bed again.

BUY YOUR COPY OF TARGET IN RANGE AT AMAZON

Em Petrova

Em Petrova was raised by hippies in the wilds of Pennsylvania but told her parents at the age of four she wanted to be a gypsy when she grew up. She has a soft spot for babies, puppies and 90s Grunge music and believes in Bigfoot and aliens. She started writing at the age of twelve and prides herself on making her characters larger than life and her sex scenes hotter than hot.

She burst into the world of publishing in 2010 after having five beautiful bambinos and figuring they were old enough to get their own snacks while she pounds away at the keys. In her not-so-spare time, she is fur-mommy to a Labradoodle named Daisy Hasselhoff.

Find More Books by Em Petrova at www.empetrova.com

Other Titles by Em Petrova

Ranger Ops
AT CLOSE RANGE
WITHIN RANGE
POINT BLANK RANGE
RANGE OF MOTION
TARGET IN RANGE
OUT OF RANGE

Knight Ops Series
ALL KNIGHTER
HEAT OF THE KNIGHT
HOT LOUISIANA KNIGHT
AFTER MIDKNIGHT
KNIGHT SHIFT
ANGEL OF THE KNIGHT
O CHRISTMAS KNIGHT

Wild West Series
SOMETHING ABOUT A LAWMAN
SOMETHING ABOUT A SHERIFF
SOMETHING ABOUT A BOUNTY HUNTER
SOMETHING ABOUT A MOUNTAIN MAN

Operation Cowboy Series
KICKIN' UP DUST
SPURS AND SURRENDER

The Boot Knockers Ranch Series
PUSHIN' BUTTONS
BODY LANGUAGE
REINING MEN
ROPIN' HEARTS
ROPE BURN
COWBOY NOT INCLUDED

The Boot Knockers Ranch Montana
COWBOY BY CANDLELIGHT
THE BOOT KNOCKER'S BABY
ROPIN' A ROMEO

Country Fever Series
HARD RIDIN'
LIP LOCK
UNBROKEN
SOMETHIN' DIRTY

Rope 'n Ride Series

BUCK

RYDER

RIDGE

WEST

LANE

WYNONNA

Rope 'n Ride On Series
JINGLE BOOTS

DOUBLE DIPPIN

LICKS AND PROMISES

A COWBOY FOR CHRISTMAS

LIPSTICK 'N LEAD

The Dalton Boys
COWBOY CRAZY Hank's story

COWBOY BARGAIN Cash's story

COWBOY CRUSHIN' Witt's story

COWBOY SECRET Beck's story

COWBOY RUSH Kade's Story

COWBOY MISTLETOE a Christmas novella

COWBOY FLIRTATION Ford's story

COWBOY TEMPTATION Easton's story

COWBOY SURPRISE Justus's story

COWGIRL DREAMER Gracie's story

COWGIRL MIRACLE Jessamine's Story

Single Titles and Boxes

STRANDED AND STRADDLED

LASSO MY HEART

SINFUL HEARTS

BLOWN DOWN

FALLEN

FEVERED HEARTS

WRONG SIDE OF LOVE

Club Ties Series

LOVE TIES

HEART TIES

MARKED AS HIS

SOUL TIES

ACE'S WILD

Firehouse 5 Series

ONE FIERY NIGHT

CONTROLLED BURN

SMOLDERING HEARTS

The Quick and the Hot Series

DALLAS NIGHTS

SLICK RIDER

SPURRED ON

EM PETROVA

WWW.EMPETROVA.COM

Made in the USA
Monee, IL
11 September 2024